WORKING
GIRL

Also by Hester Mundis

No He's Not a Monkey He's an Ape And He's My
    Son
Jessica's Wife
Separate Ways

WORKING
GIRL

HESTER MUNDIS

Coward, McCann & Geoghegan

NEW YORK

Library of Congress Cataloging in Publication Data

Mundis, Hester.
    Working girl.

    I. Title
PS3563.U454W6   1981   813'.54   81-3196
ISBN 0-698-0-11110-9   AACR2

Printed in the United States of America

This one's for Claire, with love

More and more women are starting their own businesses—to find work in a tight job market, to find freer expression of their creative and management abilities, and to put into practice their own ideas of how the business world should operate. Whatever the motives, or combination of them, the self-employed woman is an idea whose time has come.

—*Ms.*

Chapter 1

The day Sonni became a woman her father went out and bought her a pair of boxing gloves.

"What are these for?" she asked.

"Protection," Irv Mishkin said.

Sonni was confused. None of the books she'd read, nor any of her girl friends, had said anything about boxing gloves.

"I don't understand," she said.

"When in the ring, you have to know your opponent to win," Irv Mishkin said.

"Daddy, what are you talking about? Who's in the ring?"

"You are—now."

"I still don't understand."

"You will," he said.

Only years later, recalling the incident, did Sonni realize that it had been one of the few times in her father's life when he had spoken the absolute truth.

Sonni rubbed more tanning lotion on her shoulders and rolled over. The concrete around the Nackmans' pool was pebbly; even from beneath the mat it chafed her stomach. But the sun felt good and the clean Catskill breeze was tonic for her lungs, which had endured five straight days last week of New York City's worst inversion. She picked up her pencil and pulled her note pad closer.

A rape was probably just wishful thinking—the weather report said rain, and nobody got raped in the rain. With luck, there'd be an interesting mugging or a suicide; if not, she'd just have to rely on the South Bronx to come through with something. A holdup with eyewitnesses would be fine, though they could make do with a tenement fire. If worst came to worst, she supposed, a cancer update sandwiched between the strike and the current Mideast talks would suffice. She made a note of it and put down the pencil.

If she had listened to her father when she got out of college, and gone into merchandising—he said she was a natural—she'd probably be rich by now, a well-bleached blonde in a Chanel suit who made the pages of *Forbes* and *Fortune* because at thirty-four (her last birthday) she controlled an empire of department stores, or baby boutiques, or mail-order cosmetics; a chain of successes. But it was pointless to ruminate in the subjunctive. She could do that all day, and too often lately she did. She'd been telling herself that had she stayed at Durkin and Durkin advertising, she'd be an account executive now; that had she not left Nevin Arthur's PR firm, she'd be booking celebrities onto the *Today* show and receiving giant bottles of Joy at

Christmas; that had she continued as speech writer for Senator Brewer, she'd be enjoying free trips to Bermuda on private jets and dinners at the White House.

But she'd quit them all. She couldn't, she had discovered almost ruefully, stand the hype. She wanted a career with meaning, with integrity, with purpose; her own special niche. So at thirty-four she was a rangy brunette, grateful to friends for a weekend invitation to the Catskills, a stalker of Loehmann's best buys, an overworked, underpaid assignments editor and all-around towel for a second-rate producer of a third-rate TV news show.

Some niche.

Damn, but she wished she had a lover, at least one to think about. Steve, though far from a superstud, had gotten her mind off her job. But it had been three months since she'd told him to take the hypoallergenic pillow she'd bought for him and stuff it. She wasn't really sorry; it hadn't been an affair of consequence, and living alone had its advantages. Still, three months were three months. Lately she was regressing to fantasies about her ex-husband Lenny—and he wasn't even good in bed. It was depressing. Everything was depressing these days. Maybe it was her job. Then again, maybe it was her father. Him and his damn Dinky. Why couldn't he have retired like her friends' fathers?

Sonni glanced over at Andrea, who was lying on a mat beside her. Andrea's father was the same age as Sonni's and he had moved to Hawaii years ago. He called his daughter once a month to tell her how beautiful the weather was. Some people had all the luck. Not that Andrea was one of them, but she did get her fair share.

Andrea's eyes were closed and covered by two wads of damp cotton. The sun had turned her lavishly oiled skin a bright pink, and with her elbows finned out at her side she looked disquietingly like a beached salmon. But the beached salmon was smiling serenely, and Sonni knew that the only time Andrea smiled serenely was when she could fit into a size six or when she was having an affair.

Andrea Nackman was definitely not a size six.

Sonni felt a twinge of jealousy. Andrea had a new lover. It was as obvious as it always was. But then, Andrea also had a husband. Sonni felt the twinge disappear.

Bernard Nackman sat naked and abstracted in a floating pool recliner; a copy of *Variety*, dampening at the edges, discreetly covered his lap. A glass of Perrier jutted from its Styrofoam well in the float; a portable telephone rested alongside it.

"I was just thinking," he said to no one in particular, though actually addressing his wife, "that what I need to come up with is a kind of fear thing that touches everyone. You know, something primal."

"Ummm. Right," Andrea said, her eyes still closed, her serenity unruffled. The perfect producer's wife.

Andrea knew her part and played it well. She agreed with everything Bernard said whenever he said it. They rarely argued, and were it not for the fact that she had unilaterally decided to forgo fidelity as early as two weeks after their wedding, Sonni would have to admit they had a perfect marriage. Andrea's total support had given Bernard the courage to go to a major studio with his first disaster film, *Timber!*, the story of a cure for Dutch elm disease that backfires and starts an epidemic of falling trees across the parks, playgrounds, and backyards of the United States. It was low-budget, used a lot of stock documentary footage, and netted the Nackmans more than a million. Spurred on by Andrea and the rewards of cataclysm, Bernard followed *Timber!* with several other films,

which featured the aberrant behavior of a variety of ani-
mals, insects, and vegetables. Rotting wood (*Timber!*) had
bought their house, killer gnats (*The Big Buzz-off*) had
paid for their twin Mercedeses, and radioactive peanuts
(*Bet You Can't Eat Just One*) had paid for their son Dennis' orthodonture. Bernard's last two efforts, *Famine* and
Stampede, bombed at the box office. Lately, Andrea had
confided to Sonni, Bernard was running scared.

"I need something that will have them coiling round
the block for tickets, that will leave them screaming in
their sleep."

Andrea rolled over. "Right," she said.

"What I want is a fear that really gets people where
they live."

"How about death?" Sonni suggested.

"Huh?" Bernard leaned forward; some of the Perrier
spilled into the pool.

"Better yet, old age. Everyone's afraid of old age. We
all know what it leads to."

"Wait a minute, wait a min-ute," Bernard waved his
hand, sloshing more Perrier into the pool, "I think you've
got something. There could be a sudden outbreak of it. No
one knows what causes it. Babies, kids, cheerleaders, rock
stars, athletes: they all contract it, they grow old, senile,
and die within a week." He tugged thoughtfully at the
gold chain around his neck. "It has legs." He lifted the
phone and began to dial.

"Sounds great," Andrea said. She stood, pulled up the
straps on her suit. "That deserves a drink, Sonni. Come on
inside." She rolled her eyes toward the house, indicating
that she had more to offer than gin and tonic. Sonni
guessed it had something to do with the smile.

As soon as they were out of Bernard's view, Sonni's
guess proved accurate.

"Whew! Thanks. That ought to keep him on the phone to the Coast for an hour. I've been dying to talk to you alone."

"I figured as much," Sonni said, "when you asked him to go for the papers this morning."

"Really?" Andrea looked worried. "I thought it sounded perfectly normal. He usually picks up the *Times* on Sunday."

"He was still in his pajamas." Though Bernard Nackman swam, cooked, and played backgammon nude, being aggressively proud of the two thousand miles he'd put on his body since he'd begun jogging four years ago, he never slept without pajamas.

"Oh." Andrea bit her lip. "You don't think he sensed it, do you?" She liked her house, her Mercedes, her lovers, her freedom to write poems about game shows and nuclear reactors. Without Bernard she couldn't afford any of them.

"I doubt it," Sonni said. She doubted if Bernard could sense anything that didn't relate somehow to commercial cataclysm or his body.

"He may be a schmuck, but he's no dummy," Andrea said defensively. "And he's possessive as hell, believe me. When I was having that affair with Lyle, my internist, I lived in terror thinking that Bernard would find out and do something . . . well, something violent."

"Oh, come on, Andrea." Sonni fixed herself a drink.

"You don't know Bernard. He has depths. Unfathomable depths."

Sonni refrained from comment. Bernard's last shrink, a mutual friend, had once confided in unethical, inebriated confidence that Bernard Nackman was one of the most boring neurotics he'd ever met. ("His nightmares put me to sleep," he said.) If Bernard had depths, then Sonni would stick to the shallows.

She sucked the lime juice from the tips of her fingers and picked up her drink. "So, tell me. Who is it, or am I supposed to guess?"

Andrea sat down, cross-legged on the couch, hugged herself in anticipatory delight. "Guess." They had played the same game before, more times than Sonni thought it proper to remember.

"All right. Give me a moment." Sonni dropped another cube into her glass and, from the corner of her eye, caught her reflection in the ice bucket. The weekend tan was a pleasant surprise. With her overgrown permed hair it made her look athletic, as if she had closets full of tennis rackets, sweatbands, white skirts. Though fleeting, there was a nostalgic quality to the image. Sonni had vehemently renounced athletics years ago, after one of her dates couldn't decide whether he wanted to feel her up or shoot baskets with her. The only piece of sporting equipment she used now was her diaphragm—and she was even getting out of practice with that.

"Well?" Andrea pressed, eager as ever to divest her conscience of its weightless burden. She began twisting a section of her hair into a tight coil.

Sonni sipped the gin and tonic. Usually, she could figure out who Andrea was sleeping with just by sifting out the clues. They were always there. The year that Andrea chatted at length about her duodenum and argued at cocktail parties on how the government ripped off Medicaid doctors, Sonni knew it was the internist right off. The following year, when she went clematis crazy and had vines of it planted all around the house, the most obvious suspect, the guy from the nursery, was the one.

Thinking back, in only two instances was Sonni stumped: one was when Andrea was screwing another producer, which left her behaving exactly as she did when she was just screwing Bernard; the other was the time she had taken up with her ex-therapist and blocked the whole thing.

Sonni looked around the room for telltale incongruities, books that neither Andrea nor Bernard would ordinarily read, bric-a-brac that did not belong, but there was nothing.

Andrea grinned, smug, the perpetrator of a perfect crime.

Glancing out the window, Sonni noticed a large pile of old shingles. "And what's that?" she asked, raising an indicting eyebrow.

"Oh, that?" Andrea lit a cigarette. "Just our old roof. We're having the section over our bedroom redone."

"Hmmm. Who's putting on the new roof?"

"A local. Nice kid. Twenty-five, big, honest, reliable."

"Good in bed?"

"Unbelievable!" Andrea jumped up and hugged Sonni. "I've got to tell you, this is the craziest thing I've ever gotten into."

"I doubt it. I still remember your fling with that guy at the Seaquarium who wanted the dolphins to watch."

"You mean Fred?" Andrea laughed. "God, Sonni, that was years ago. This is totally different."

"One hopes."

"Oh, it is. Really." Andrea hooked her arm through her friend's. "I mean when you take away the fact that I'm theoretically old enough to be his mother, that philosophically, socially, and economically we have nothing in common, it becomes clear that we have something special."

"Good sex."

"That too."

"Too? What else?"

"Don't be such a Capricorn. There's more to this affair than sex. Believe me."

Sonni didn't, but there was no point in saying so. Andrea said the same thing about all her affairs. With the man from the nursery Andrea had called it "a mutual appreciation of earth's fecundities," which meant that after they both came they would discuss the weed-destroying merits of pachysandra, or the two-year wait for harvesting asparagus. Sonni cast a quick glance out the window to make sure Bernard was still in the pool. "So you and—"

"Henry-John," Andrea said. "Isn't that a great name?"

Sonni passed on the question. "So you and Henry-John have something together that you and Bernard don't— and it's not sex."

"I didn't say it *wasn't*, I said it was *more* than." Andrea sounded testy.

"Okay, I give up. Tell me."

"Primitive poetry."

"Primitive poetry?" Sonni repeated it slowly.

"He says things in ways that reach me on levels no one has ever reached before. I mean they turn on my soul."

No doubt her body as well, Sonni thought, though Andrea would never admit it. As a former St. Louis debutante, Andrea, for all her infidelities, had always been above Getting Laid.

"What sort of things?" Sonni asked.

"Primal. Real. They're not like the lines you get from guys on the make. I mean, when he wants something, he says so. None of those hmmm-mmms or faster or slower breathing for him. If he wants me to go down on him, he doesn't just keep pressing the top of my head until I get the idea. He says it straight out: 'Suck my dork.' If he wants it faster, he says, '*faster.*' I mean the whole thing is totally honest. He's the first man I've met who doesn't pretend concern about my orgasm. And it's refreshing, healthy." She paused for a moment. "Wholesome."

It sounded as if she were talking about goat's milk instead of sex. Sonni drained her drink and fixed another. Andrea continued to enumerate Henry-John's atavistic charms, while her husband floated naked and out of earshot in the pool.

Sonni listened more out of politeness than interest. All her friends seemed to be in heat lately. Every damn one of them was having an affair, and (not inconceivably because she herself wasn't) their reasons, rationalizations, and gripes had begun to take on rather irksome similarities. "But this time it's different," they'd say. And it never was. It was like her father complaining about eating hamburgers every night and then going out for dinner at McDonald's.

Andrea's fling with the roofer, no matter how she protested its uniqueness, was a replay of all her others. It had, Sonni felt, very little to do with pheromones, grand passion, or poetry, and a lot to do with boredom. While Andrea praised Bernard's bedroom performance highly (once claiming to have gone through a month of lovemaking without repeating the same act twice), she resented his passion for golf, especially his getting out of bed to putt after sex, and doing it with Bernard was still just doing it with Bernard. Whenever someone else appeared in her life she convinced herself that she was being deprived of some nameless happiness and was . . . entitled. However uninspired the affair turned out to be, it was nonetheless a new sexual experience and she was having it—and not with Bernard.

Andrea was still rhapsodizing Henry-John's primal essence, which appeared to be his penchant for belching and breaking wind unselfconsciously, when Sonni noticed Bernard paddling his float toward the pool ladder.

"I think Bernard's coming," she said.

"Damn. I wanted to tell you about the hang glider."

"What hang glider?"

"The one I'm buying for Henry-John."

"They cost a fortune. That's crazy!"

Andrea shook her head. "It's love."

"That's what you said when you bought the Aqualung for What's-His-Name—"

"Fred. God, Sonni, that was *different.*"

"I still say you're crazy."

"You sound like my first therapist." Andrea's first therapist had been a deranged Jungian who believed that all his patients were crazy, pinning television emissions as the cause. He'd convinced most of them to discard their sets, and a good dozen to commit themselves, before he himself was taken away. Andrea had given her own TV to her cleaning lady, an elderly German woman who two weeks later dumped the contents of her medicine cabinet into a beer stein and killed herself.

"Really, you're too sensible," Andrea said disdainfully, as if accusing Sonni of gaucherie. "You've got to get out into the real world more often. Get away from that news program. It's draining your womanly juices."

Andrea was only partly right, the *Nightly News* was draining Sonni completely. It was reminding her more and more every day of her father's novelty business with its calculated manipulation of the public. When marbles were popular, her father had bought the cheapest, dipped them in glitter, and sold them for five times the price. When coverage of a young actress's jump from the George Washington Bridge had bolstered ratings, the *Nightly News* ran a month-long retrospective on famous suicides. Glitter Marbles and old suicides—if they paid the rent and pleased the advertisers, what difference did ethics make? It distressed Sonni, increased her anxiety about not having a career she believed in, a place in the business world that she could call her own. Most of all, and what she didn't like to admit, she felt she was a disappointment to her father.

"We've got a goddam gorilla!" Bernard boomed as he entered, clutching his portable telephone and draped in a Gucci towel. His rubber thongs slapped the floor, made the sound of a small child clapping, as he went to the bar.

Andrea sprang to his side like an automatic latch. "Oh, darling, that's wonderful." She kissed his stylishly grayed temple.

Bernard Nackman, whose forehead was receding at a rate correlative to his ambition, had his hair ministered to at an exclusive salon three thousand miles away on Rodeo Drive that specialized in transplants and coloring. Too impatient for transplants, he had decided to enhance his remaining hair with silver wings that flared out behind each ear. They had been designed, he'd told Sonni, to look like the wings on Mercury's ankles. He'd said that just having it done gave him more get-up-and-go.

"David loved the idea, loved it." He kissed the portable phone and laid it on the bar. He poured himself a Scotch.

"Bernardo, that's just marvelous," Andrea cooed. "I'm so happy." She flung her arms around his neck and hugged him, loosening the towel, which fell open and hung, like Bernard, limply between them. Sonni studied the lime in her glass.

Bernard rewrapped himself and sat down on a barstool. "I tell you, I never heard David sound so enthused."

"That's great, dear. But remember, David's known for his initial enthusiasm. They don't call him the Doberman of Beverly Hills for nothing."

"I know, but this was different."

"I'm sure," Andrea assured him without assurance.

"The whole idea of rock stars and child actors getting pathetically old really got to him. He saw it as box-office poignant, a three-handkerchief thriller: wants to call it *Terminal*." Bernard bit his lip and fiddled with one of his chains. "What do you think?"

"I think it's a helluva title," Andrea said.

Bernard screwed up his face. "I don't like it."

"Me neither," said Andrea quickly. A perfect hundred-and-eighty-degree turn. "I meant that would be a helluva poor title for a film."

"But on the other hand," Bernard mused, "it's not bad."

"That's true, too. It's not bad."

"But it's not good."

Andrea shook her head. "Not good."

Sonni checked her watch. "I think I'd better get my stuff together. I want to catch the seven-thirty bus back to the city."

"Sure." Bernard thrummed his fingers abstractedly on the bar. "But it's not bad. Not bad at all."

Andrea shook her head. "No. Not bad."

"But not good."

Andrea made a face. "Not good."

"What do you think, Sonni?" Bernard asked, a moot question since he had about as much interest in other people's opinions as he had in their shoe sizes.

"I don't think it's bad," she said, "but I don't think it's good either."

"That's just how I feel," he said, sincerely surprised.

"Me too," said Andrea. The Greek chorus.

They both looked pleased, as if something had been resolved. Sonni wished she could handle tomorrow's broadcast that easily, to say nothing of her father's Dinky. She excused herself and went to pack.

When she returned, Bernard was pacing the room. He was still in his towel, now wrapped sarong fashion. He fondled his portable telephone as he paced. Andrea stood in the doorway, the car keys in her hand. She picked up Sonni's bag.

"When Bernard is creating, I don't like to disturb him," she said softly, but loud enough for him to hear. "When he's conceiving a film, he can't think of anything else."

Bernard, who'd been facing the window, turned around. "When's that roofer going to get that goddam pile of shingles out of here?"

"Tomorrow," Andrea said quickly.

"Looks like shit," Bernard grumbled.

"It sure does," Andrea said.

"Why didn't he dump them right into his truck?"

"Good question," said Andrea.

"Asshole kid."

To her credit, Andrea said nothing.

On the ride to the bus, Andrea said. "I'm picking up the hang glider for Henry-John tomorrow. I had to give my butcher's brother ten bucks so he'd come with me. He has a license. You can't get those things without one, did you know that?"

"No, but it seems to me that you're going through an awful lot of trouble for just another—"

"He's not just another. He's unique, a primitive poet, a free spirit. I want him to have the opportunity to fly like a bird."

Sonni had an unpleasant vision of free-spirited Henry-John jumping off the cliffs at New Paltz, belching and farting his way to disaster.

"He could get hurt, you know," Sonni said.

"Every affair has its risks."

Chapter 2

The Trailways bus was already crowded. Sonni paused at the driver's seat and scanned the passengers. It was a two-and-a-half hour ride from Woodstock to New York, and she'd be damned if she was going to sit next to some old lady who wanted to unburden herself to a stranger; on the trip up she'd gotten a detailed account of a daughter-in-law who refused to use disposable diapers and the bizarre particulars of a misdiagnosed case of shingles. Why was it that on a public conveyance people often felt, simply because they were going in the same direction, that they had something in common with you?

She didn't want to be saddled with a talker. She wanted to be alone, to think. It was unfair to punish people who took public transportation by making them travel in pairs.

She walked down the aisle slowly, intent upon the business of finding a silent partner.

A gray-haired man, looking somewhat annoyed at having to wait for the new arrivals, sat on the left. His head was turned toward the window, but Sonni could see that his lips were set tight. They were definitely not lips from which trivia fell. Expletives perhaps, or commands, but certainly not domestic complaints.

Sonni found a place on the overhead rack for her suitcase and was preparing to sit down when she was suddenly shoved forward.

"Excuse me," said a woman holding two shopping bags, and she thrust herself into the seat.

"I beg your pardon," Sonni said, "but—"

"That's quite all right." The woman smiled dismissively. She was fiftyish and bosomy, with a Nixon ski-sloped nose and hair the color of rusty Brillo. She wore a bright green T-shirt which said: "What's Mine Is Yours."

"Look, madam, I was going to sit—"

"Beat it, tootsie," the woman said from the corner of her mouth. She turned toward the man and began fumbling with her packages. "I do hope these won't be in your way, sir." Her blue eyelashes fluttered like the wings of an insect preparing to mate.

The man acknowledged her with a grimace. He would have been perfect, but the T-shirted woman was formidably inert and determinedly in rut. Sonni was in no mood for a hassle.

She spotted an empty seat toward the rear, next to a man in his late thirties. He didn't immediately strike her as silent, but he was good-looking; after three dateless months, that was definitely a meliorating factor. When she reached the seat she saw that his large canvas bag and jacket were on it, along with the complete Sunday *Times,* nonverbal bus communication for "I want to be alone."

She also saw that he was deeply engrossed in the instructions on a nasal-spray package.

"Do you mind if I sit here?" she asked.

His head snapped up. "Wha-huh?" He looked startled and vaguely annoyed, as if he'd been jarred from an engrossing passage in *War and Peace.* "Oh . . . sure," he said, and put the canvas bag on the floor. He tossed his jacket and the *Times* on the overhead rack, then sat back down and resumed reading the nasal-spray package.

Sonni adjusted her seat to a more comfortable position. The bus hissed and started to move.

"Jeezus!" the man muttered angrily. He tossed the box into his canvas bag and stared sullenly out the window.

Sonni wondered if she should have respected his nonverbal communication. Anyone who had an emotional response to a nasal-spray package was a precarious seat partner, no matter what he looked like.

Out of the corner of her eye, she reaffirmed her first impression. He was handsome. Blond and blue-eyed, he had that permanent-pressed quality one associated with lifeguards and storm troopers. He wore an ordinary blue chambray shirt, and no chains or rings. It was refreshing to think he might be straight. Unconsciously, she fluffed her hair.

The long bus ride was the perfect opportunity for her to consider the sales potential of her father's latest novelty as well as to plan tomorrow's broadcast, yet she wanted to forget both. She wanted to forget about everything, even about wanting a lover, which reminded her that she'd forgotten to pick up batteries for her vibrator.

She cast another sidelong glance at her seat partner. He

was still staring out the window. For all that she'd read about body language, his posture told her nothing; she couldn't even work up a diverting fantasy. Reluctantly she took out her scheduling notes. The news was vital; her father's Dinky could wait.

Actually, Irving Mishkin's Dinky couldn't wait, and Sonni knew it, which made concentrating on her notes even more difficult. If her father was to be believed, his business, maybe his whole future, rested on that goddam Dinky. And all it was was a glamorized Hula-Hoop. She'd even told him so last week.

"But it's a million-dollar novelty, Son," he'd protested.

Sonni had winced. She always winced when her father addressed her that way. Her name was Sonora, which was difficult enough to live with. Blanche and Irving Mishkin had been in Mexico when she was born, between Guadalajara and Sonora. Fortunately they had decided to name their baby after Blanche's late sister Selma and therefore needed an S. If they had decided to name her after Irving's Aunt Gussie, she could have gone through life as Guadalajara.

Irv Mishkin had taken to calling his daughter Son twenty-five years ago. Up to that point she had been only Sonni, Princess, and Daddy's Girl, pampered with dolls, toy stoves, tea sets, bubbly bath salts, and other obeisances to nascent femininity. But when she was seven, her mother's uterus, obstinately infertile since Sonni's birth, had been summarily dismissed. Her father never recovered.

The doctor, Wilton "Knife" Fiedler, as Irv Mishkin called him, was prone to overreacting to abdominal pains. His comment to Blanche Mishkin when she awoke after her surprise hysterectomy was, "I'd rather be safe than sorry." Sonni's mother, a self-taught optimist and born spelunker, took the news in stride; her husband was devastated. His dream of a scion for his novelty and *tchotchke* business was shattered. He firmly believed that it was a man's world, and to Make It Big in that world you had to be one, work like one, or at least think like one. The realization that his *only* child might be denied the Brass Ring of Success because of genetic chance was unacceptable. He threw out Sonni's dolls, tea sets, and Mary Janes and replaced them with trucks, penknives, and sneakers. He took her to ball games and on fishing trips. He slapped her back a lot.

He called her Son.

He also called her for advice, and money. To launch his Disco Dinky he wanted her okay and three grand.

"It's worth a million."

"It's another Hula-Hoop."

"It's . . . an idea whose time has come." For Irv Mishkin, these six words were as sacred as *broche*, a blessing that had become *the* tenet of his faith in the American Dream. As far back as Sonni could remember, he had pressed this dogma upon her: *If you find an idea whose time has come, the world is your clamshell.* For him it was an unshakable truth; for her it held about as much meaning as Hickory, Dickory, Dock.

"But, Dad, it's still a Hula-Hoop," Sonni said wearily.

"It's different. It has tiny rubber roller skates. When it hits the floor it spins around. Get it going and it bounces up and down you like a ring on a piston." He made a circle with his fingers and moved it back and forth over his thumb.

"Who cares about rings and pistons?" She averted her eyes as her father continued his illustration.

"Henry Ford did, and look where it got him."

Sonni rolled her eyes.

Irv Mishkin tossed up Henry Ford, Jay Gould, and Charles Goodyear the way other parents did Abe Lincoln, George Washington, and Jesus Christ. Self-made millionaires were his gurus. He believed in the transcendental Power of Money.

The Dinky was Irv Mishkin's new ticket to Nirvana. Nirvana for Sonni's father was a condominium in Fort Lauderdale, unlimited credit in Las Vegas, a box at Shea Stadium, and a humidor the size of a redwood filled with Havana cigars.

He puffed on a twenty-five-cent White Owl as he spoke. "Look, Son, I don't want to sell this idea to a manufacturer yet. They'll buy it cheap, sell it cheap, it'll come off like just another Hula-Hoop."

"But that's what it is."

"Dammit, it's a Dinky. A Disco Dinky. I've got a guy in Taiwan right now who can make them in all colors and stud them with rhinestones for seventy-three cents apiece!"

"Rhinestones?"

Irv Mishkin shifted the cigar to the corner of his mouth, clamped it with his teeth. "I want," he said proudly, "for it to become a plaything of the rich."

"But, Dad—"

"There's a lot of rich people in this country, believe you me."

"There are a lot more who aren't."

"You're telling me?"

"But then wouldn't it make more sense to—"

Irv Mishkin put his arm around his daughter's shoulders. "Son, Son," he said, shaking his head, "I'm afraid you just don't have the genes for business."

"Genes have nothing to do with it," Sonni said impa-

tiently. "Nidetch made millions from Weight Watch-
ers."

"Luck."

"Oh, come on, Dad."

He patted Sonni's shoulder. "Face it, business is a man's
game, and it's a man's world."

"I give up," Sonni sighed.

"See?" Irv poked a finger at her chest. "A man
wouldn't say that." He smiled. Sonni didn't.

"Hey, what's that?" He punched her arm affectionate-
ly.

"Stop that," Sonni said, annoyed.

Irv Mishkin made a fist and pretended to jab at her.
"You used to have a pretty good right hook when you
were eleven," he said.

"Please, Dad."

He held up his palms. "Okay. No reminiscing. Let's talk
business. I know the Dinky can do it."

"You said that about the disposable ashtrays."

"That was different."

"That was two thousand dollars."

"I've got plans for the Dinky," Irv persisted. "I'm going
to launch it with a celebrity campaign. I'm sending complimentary Dinkies to Margaret Trudeau, Prince Charles,
Bianca Jagger, and a couple of others."

Sonni had difficulty imagining Bianca Jagger twirling a
Dinky. It didn't seem quite right for Prince Charles either.

"If the Dinky makes it," Irv Mishkin told her, "I'm on
easy street. If it doesn't, I'm on welfare."

"There's no need to be dramatic."

"Dramatic? It's the truth. I still don't understand why
your mother, may she rest in peace, did that." By "that"

he meant Blanche Mishkin's last will and testament, which decreed that the money from all her Christmas Club accounts, which she regularly opened at any bank offering a giveaway to new depositors, would be left to her daughter in trust for her husband. Though a modest sum, being the earnings from Blanche's lectures on spelunking at colleges, churches, and B'nai B'rith meetings, by the time Sonni was twenty-one it amounted to more than nineteen thousand dollars. Sonni's father had already gone through half of it.

"Momma wanted to do what would be best for you in the long run."

"Well, then I think I should get the money soon. I'm not so far from the finish line."

Sonni told him she'd think about it.

She had tried not to think about it all weekend. She was still trying as the bus turned onto the Thruway.

The man next to her bent over and, reaching into his canvas bag, took out a familiar pink box. He turned it around, examined all six sides, then began to read it.

Sonni recognized the box because she had one just like it in her bathroom cabinet. It contained a disposable douche.

She forgot about Margaret Trudeau, Prince Charles, and Bianca Jagger gyrating with her father's Dinkies. She forgot about tomorrow night's broadcast. She was fascinated.

"Damn!" the man muttered. He slammed the box against his knee, which slammed against hers. He said, "Excuse me."

"That's quite all right," said Sonni.

"Damn!" he muttered again.

"Is something wrong?" she asked.

"*Wrong?*" The word clanged like a Japanese gong.

Two people turned to stare. He repeated it softly, but with no less anger. "Wrong?"

Obviously something was. Sonni had serious misgivings about her query, felt that whatever was troubling the box reader she didn't want to know. She smiled weakly. "I didn't mean to pry."

"Read this," he said angrily.

Sonni leaned over. The disposable douche, which the manufacturer claimed was "Nature's Formula Scented With The Fragrance Of A Dozen Roses," appeared perfectly ordinary. She didn't know what she was supposed to read. She tried the roses.

"That's bad enough," he said. "Perfume and D and C Red Number Nineteen. But it's *this* that really gets me. I mean, where do they come off saying they have the proper pH balance for your vagina?" He pointed at Sonni.

Sonni opened her mouth but could think of absolutely nothing to say.

"Look," he said earnestly, "you seem intelligent. Do *you* know what the acid–alkaline balance of your vagina should be?"

"Uh, no. I can't say that I do."

"How many women do you think might?"

"I . . . I don't suppose too many." Sonni began to feel uncomfortable. Why was this man so concerned with the pH of women's vaginas?

"I'd feel safe saying almost none," he said confidently.

"I don't think you'd be far wrong."

"Wyatt Stelson," he said, smiled.

"I beg your pardon?"

He put out his hand. Sonni shook it, only then realizing he'd given his name. And only then realizing that though he looked nothing like what she thought he looked like, she knew him; that many women who didn't know the pH of their vaginas knew him. His name was virtually a household word.

Wyatt Stelson was America's most zealous new consumer advocate. He picked up where Nader and his Raiders left off—or rather, picked on what Nader and his Raiders didn't bother with. He called himself the People's Person, and his goal, as he'd told the New York *Times* last year, was "Truth in everything." He was the nemesis of copywriters from coast to coast. He was hated by publishers. He was the scourge of Madison Avenue.

He rose to fame on a typo.

The typo was an *e* that should have been an *i*. It appeared in a blurb on a paperback book. The book was about Plato, Marx, Shakespeare, Sukarno, George Washington Carver, and Kissinger. It was called *Movers and Shakers*. The blurb on *Movers and Shakers* listed the names and then said something to the effect of "six lives that changed the world." It was in the word "six" that the *e* replaced the *i*.

Wyatt Stelson claimed that the book enjoyed a brisk sale to which it was not entitled, that it promised readers more than it delivered. The publisher said at the trial that the company would correct the error in future printings. But Stelson wasn't satisfied. He was convinced that a work on Sukarno and George Washington Carver would never have a second printing because he'd written one, *The Greats*, the only book ever to be remaindered before publication date.

The publisher of *Movers and Shakers* was forced to recall it at a cost of several hundred thousand dollars, and the brouhaha put Wyatt Stelson on *Good Morning, America*. There, on the air, when asked if he planned to make a career of punishing publishers, he said, "I have bigger fish to fry."

Lakeland Fish Sticks was his first big fish fry. He demanded that they either prove they used none but the "perkiest perch in the sea" or drop the phrase from their ads. It was a small consumer victory for Stelson, but it deep-sixed Lakeland Fish Sticks.

He caused another furor when he decided to go after breakfast cereals; an even larger one when he went after the American Pharmaceutical Association and referred to all drugs that didn't sting, burn, or make you want to throw up as illicit. It seemed to Sonni, as she shook his hand, somewhat of a comedown for the People's Person to be getting into nasal sprays and ladies' douches.

"Sonni Rubin," she said. "I'm very pleased to meet you."

"Same here." He flashed a charming smile.

"You don't look anything like your photographs."

"I know. I can't afford to in my line. If everyone knew what I looked like I'd never be treated as a typical consumer. I make all my public appearances in a dark wig and glasses."

"I guess that's why I didn't recognize you."

"I would have been upset if you had."

Sonni felt the conversation waning and realized that she didn't want it to. She pointed to the douche box. "You seemed pretty upset about that a few moments ago." It was like throwing another log on the fire.

Wyatt gripped the box as if it were a hand grenade. "It's this kind of crap that shouldn't be foisted upon consumers."

"Douches?" Sonni asked, confused.

"Untruths."

"You mean the manufacturer is lying about the stuff?"

"Not being honest is a better way to put it."

"Isn't that the same thing?"

"Not exactly," Wyatt said, his blue eyes glinting with purpose. Sonni noticed that he had a dimple. "Millions of people are being suckered in every day because they're unaware of dishonest honesty. Things like this." He waved the box in the air. Sonni averted her eyes.

"Thousands of women think this stuff actually *does* something for their vagina, just because it smells like roses. If it were really Nature's Formula it wouldn't smell like roses."

Sonni could offer no argument. Wyatt put the box away, took out a can of fruit punch, and began reading.

Sonni pretended to return to her notes. She pretended because at the moment concentration on unions, nuclear reactors, and the garbage strike was impossible. She couldn't deal with realities. She had a face for her fantasies: Wyatt Stelson. The first man to offer any promise of a relationship she might find meaningful.

She wondered what he looked like naked.

She wondered how she could get him to take her to bed.

She wondered if other women wondered things like that about men they barely knew.

Three months were three months; she leaned back and did a lot of wondering.

As the bus approached New York City, she realized that they hadn't spoken for forty-five minutes. She wondered if she'd blown it.

Wyatt was looking out the window.

"Don't you love that skyline?" she asked, hoping to reengage him.

"Yes." He didn't even turn around.

It was like trying to start an old Fiat on a rainy day. Not even a sputter.

When they entered the Lincoln Tunnel and he still hadn't spoken, Sonni was totally dejected and felt she had nothing to lose by being forward.

She purposefully let her broadcast notes slip into his lap.

"Oh, I'm terribly sorry," she said, not knowing quite how to reclaim them.

He gathered them together.

"Thank you . . . Um . . . I guess you must be used to handling lots of papers." The inanity of her own words caused her cheeks to flush.

"I don't make small talk," he said.

"Excuse me?"

"I don't make small talk. Some people think I'm rude, but words without relevance are just another form of dishonest honesty for me. I say what I have to say, what I want to say, when it's time to say it."

"I see," she said, noticing that his eyes were actually more indigo than blue.

"I read a situation, evaluate it, then deal with it as openly and honestly as possible."

"That's admirable."

"Timing is everything," he said, and looked at his watch.

The bus was just pulling into the terminal.

"Will you have dinner with me, and afterwards sex?"

Sonni was so taken aback she could barely sputter, "What?"

"Please don't act offended, unless you really are. You and I both know that men don't take attractive women they've just met out to dinner without thoughts of sex. Why not be up front about it?"

Why not? Sonni knew she could think of a few reasons if she tried, but she didn't want to try. The thought of going to bed with Wyatt Stelson obliterated rationality, morality, tomorrow night's broadcast, and, thank God, her father's Dinky.

"Why not?" she said, wondering if the People's Person would be upset if she smelled like roses.

Chapter 3

Wyatt took her to a French restaurant on West Forty-eighth Street. He liked the restaurant, he said, because it was the only one in New York where the menu was printed entirely in English.

"No *veau, boeuf,* or *poisson* here," he said. "A guy doesn't have to pay fifty bucks to point at a menu like a schmuck because he can't pronounce something." He then proceeded to order a chopped steak, medium rare, in perfect French.

When Sonni appeared surprised, he told her he spoke four languages fluently. "Just because I'm the People's Person," he said, "doesn't mean I'm your average Joe."

Sonni ordered what was listed as a "cheese and bacon pie."

"*Un quiche*," Wyatt said with aplomb.

The waiter wrote the order on a small green pad with two quick flourishes—the flourishes were the numbers 3 and 5. Then he brought the wine.

Sonni did most of the talking during dinner. Wyatt limited himself to such relevancies as "Please pass the salt," "More wine?," and "May I have the butter?" He did tell her, though, that he was leaving for France the following day to see what he could do about Anglicizing wine labels. "You shell out twelve bucks for a bottle and you don't know what the hell you're getting," he said. "At least California and New York wines give you the straight story. What do construction workers in Cleveland know about *appellation controlée* when they want a bottle of Château Latour?"

Very little, Sonni suspected, though she couldn't imagine a large demand for Château Latour from construction workers, especially in Cleveland. She told Wyatt that he'd set himself a hefty task.

Wyatt told her he worked best under pressure.

He also told her that he was underpaid for what he did, that he'd once been locked in a refrigerator, and that he'd been married twice to the same woman. "The first time we divorced it was because we didn't know what we wanted. The second time it was because we did."

After that he said only two things, one to the waiter and one to Sonni. Both were relevant. To the waiter he said, "*L'addition, s'il vous plaît,*" and flashed an American Express card. To Sonni he said, "Your place or mine?"

Sonni's apartment was in an architecturally uninspired building on East Ninth Street called the Palladian. It was squat and plain by Manhattan standards, and nobody famous lived in it, though Al Pacino was the cousin of a speech therapist in 2-B and had paid a condolence call last

year when the speech therapist's father died. It had a ten-
ants' committee, but the meetings were always being can-
celed, and it remained one of the few buildings in the area
that no one bothered trying to co-op.

Two doormen were employed by the landlord. They
worked in shifts around the clock to ward off muggers,
unauthorized deliveries, and nonresident trick-or-treaters.
Their names were John and Bill. John and Bill wore gray
uniforms and caps that made them look like Confederate
soldiers and were apparently narcoleptic. One or the other
was usually slouched in a chair in the lobby, no matter
what the hour, dead out.

Sonni was surprised to see Bill shake himself awake to
open the door when she and Wyatt arrived. She was even
more surprised when Bill took her suitcase and carried it
to the elevator. It was something he usually did only before Christmas.

"Why, thank you," she said.

"That's okay. It'll be Bill Spitz's last time, anyway." He
always referred to himself in the third person.

"Are you leaving?" Sonni asked.

"Yep. Bill Spitz is going into politics."

"Politics?"

"You don't get noplace in this world by being a doorman. But if Bill Spitz was a legislator, a congressman, or a
senator, he could be President or something."

"That's true," Wyatt said. It was relevant.

"Thank you," said Bill. He pressed the elevator button.

"I didn't know you were interested in politics," Sonni
said. She had never even known he could walk.

"Bill Spitz watches the elections on TV every year."

"I see," said Sonni, wishing the elevator would come.

"Besides," he said, "Bill Spitz knows how to talk to

people. Poor people. He knows their concerns and how to get their vote. Poor people don't care about war in the Middle East, the price of gold, the national deficit. They got their own problems. Bill Spitz knows this and can get their vote. He can win by a landslide."

"How?" Wyatt asked.

The elevator arrived and Sonni stepped in. Wyatt held the door, waited for Bill's answer.

"By promising them the things they really want—new stereos, video games for the kids, paint jobs for their cars. You know, stuff they can relate to."

"But how are you going to accomplish that?"

"What's that have to do with getting elected?"

"But you'll be promising things you can't deliver."

"You ever know a successful politician who didn't?"

"But . . . but that's immoral."

"Hey, man, Bill Spitz wants to be a politician, not the Pope."

Sonni prayed as she reached for the light switch that she hadn't left the apartment a mess. She had enough right now just dealing with her own appearance without having to make excuses for her apartment.

She couldn't tell what sort of impression Wyatt had of her, but she feared the worst. Sure, lots of women went to bed with guys after a first date without seeming . . . loose. But to agree beforehand was an entirely different matter. Not that Sonni assigned sex the towering significance it received from books, films, the Church, and Middle America. She didn't. Actually, she had a rather sporting attitude about it—mostly because of her father.

Irv Mishkin had presented the facts of life very casually. He presented them to Sonni when she was ten, in the bleachers of Yankee Stadium during a Yankee–Red Sox game, during the seventh-inning stretch.

He told her that everything was quite natural. It was like a baseball game, he explained. It all depended whose side you were on. Men and women were two different teams, just like the Yankees and the Red Sox. He made men the Yankees.

Kissing was "getting to first base," petting "a double." "Third base" was everything short of intercourse, and a "home run" was scoring. He told her that everyone was genetically programmed for scoring, that it was as normal as the desire to scratch an itch. There were some people who went around scratching all the time, but they were "in another league." When she asked if the Red Sox ever got to bat, he told her that wasn't how the game was played.

Tonight she had pregame jitters. Anticipation unnerved her. She was uneasy before important lunch dates, a wreck on Christmas Eve, and fluky as a captive panda when sex was imminent.

While she made drinks, Wyatt inspected her food cabinet. He made a disparaging remark about her brand of spaghetti, then told her that the rice she was using had been found to contain a high percentage of miscellaneous small-animal waste. She wasn't up to mustering a defense of her farinaceous products; she brought the drinks into the bedroom.

Sonni relaxed in her bedroom. It was familiar, safe, reminded her of the room she grew up in. In fact, except for the absence of a Midwood High School pennant on the closet door and the presence of a double bed, the room was a fairly accurate replica of her sleep-and-study childhood sanctuary—right down to the red-white-and-blue striped bedsheets. (When she married Lenny, she'd bought the same sheets for their water bed, but put them away when Lenny had complained that they looked like a flag and made him feel as if he were being buried at sea.) Shelves—packed with books, records, magazines, and mementos—flanked her old desk, on which stood the fluorescent study lamp she'd had since junior high. Above the desk on a bulletin board was a matchbook snapshot of her mother and father at the Copacabana, two birthday cards, and her last month's Visa statement.

On the narrow wall between her windows, gathering dust, was a pair of boxing gloves.

"I see you're ready for action," Wyatt said.

Sonni flushed, not because of what he'd said but because he hadn't been the first to say it. It was apparently a common male response to boxing gloves in a woman's bedroom.

"They were a present from my father," she explained. "When I was ten."

"An odd gift for a ten-year-old girl."

"Not if she happened to be the featherweight champion of P.S. 192."

"You?"

"It was a long time ago," Sonni said, wanting to drop the subject. "I hung them up when I was twelve. I liked the way they looked."

She kicked off her shoes. It was nearly midnight. She had to be at the studio by eight-thirty tomorrow morning, and Mondays were always hell. It was time to get the ball game under way.

Sonni put the drinks on the bureau and dimmed the light. She unzipped her skirt, letting it fall to the floor. Wyatt watched her with reassuring interest. Carefully putting his wallet and watch on the night table, he unbuttoned his shirt.

Bare-chested, shirt in one hand, he drew beside her and stroked her thigh with two fingers. He asked her for a hanger.

She got him one. While he was turned away she slipped out of her blouse and panties and under the striped sheets.

Wyatt kept his back to her as he removed his pants and shorts. "Do you mind if I switch one of your skirts and use a wooden hanger? These are my traveling clothes." He told her that he had to catch a plane for Paris early in the morning and didn't want his clothes to look as if they'd been traveled in.

"Sure." Sonni gazed with libidinous interest at his back. It was tanned and surprisingly well muscled, with a cleft down the center as marked as the Continental Divide. The tan ended abruptly at his buttocks, which were a disconcerting naked white.

She wanted him to turn around. Her blatant eagerness humiliated her, but it did not diminish. She wanted to see him. Undeniably she was thinking about what all men suspected women thought about, what most women denied they even fleetingly cared about, what she herself knew from experience had little to do with sexual pleasure, sexual release, love, marriage, procreation, or even, for that matter, a good ball game. She was thinking about *size*.

The major difference between a Yankee and a Red Sox had intrigued Sonni since she'd first seen a drawing of it in a book, initially mistaking it for a poor cartographic rendering of Florida. Her confusion was dispelled at fourteen when her friend Sheryl Roseman's brother Marvin tried to get her to run her palm up and down his coastline. He was only sixteen, but his peninsula was impressive. As a Yankee, he was a veritable Babe Ruth.

Sonni later realized that it was impossible to predict any Yankee's size before a game. It was always a surprise. Some of the tallest, most muscular she'd known had the least to play with. She accepted that as nature's way of making everyone a good sport.

She felt a stab of disappointment as Wyatt turned and advanced toward the bed. She regretted having thought about Marvin Roseman. Though surging with enthusiasm, Wyatt Stelson was strictly a rookie.

He kneeled on the bed. Sonni smiled, reached up and grasped him. She reminded herself it was how the game was played that counted. An hour later she and Wyatt were asleep, exhausted and content with two dazzling home runs.

The alarm rang at seven and Wyatt was gone. Sonni was shocked. Things like that happened in movies and books, but not in real life, certainly not in hers. Never had she been unaware of someone leaving her bed. It was as if her consciousness had somehow betrayed her. If she could no longer be aware of something like that, how could she trust herself with other things? How could she be sure she turned off the gas? Paid the phone bill? Put in her diaphragm? It was unnerving. It dealt her confidence a blow to the solar plexis.

She sat up in bed and forced herself to remember what had gone on the night before. Her confidence returned when she found she could account for nearly every turn their lovemaking had taken, as well as the imaginative maneuvers that prompted both orgasms. It was no mean feat of recall; the People's Person had the sexual attention of a mayfly, devoting little more than a minute to any one form of stimulation. She couldn't remember being in that many positions in so short a time since she'd attempted to do Miss Craig's 12-day Shape-Up Program in three.

Then she saw the note. It was on the night table, hastily written on the inside of a gum wrapper. It said: *"Thanks. Great. A night worth a million. W."*

Alongside the note was something else. It was partially hidden by the base of the lamp, but totally recognizable. It was a hundred-dollar bill.

Sonni picked it up and stared at it. *What the . . .?* Then she reread the gum wrapper, held them both together.

"Why, that . . . I don't believe it!" she said aloud, comprehension barreling down on her like a Metroliner. She stared at Ben Franklin. "I don't believe it. He thought I was a professional!"

Ben Franklin smiled inscrutably. "A night worth a million, huh? What is this, a down payment?" She threw the bill on the bed and began to fume. She paced the room. So all that honesty and up-front business was a sham. He'd thought she was a hooker all along. He hadn't evidenced the slightest curiosity about what she did because he was probably convinced that he knew. No wonder he'd wrung her into all those positions—the bastard simply wanted his money's worth.

She picked up the pillow and punched it across the room.

"Damn Yankees!" she muttered.

Chapter 4

"Where's your team spirit today?" Rob Carey asked, handing Sonni a cup of coffee. She took it and brushed past him. Rob Carey was WCBN's weekend sports announcer, the son of star quarterback Vince Carey, a colorful Dallas Cowboy blinded at the height of his career by an overzealous cheerleader's baton. On Saturday and Sunday nights a cult of his father's fans would tune in to watch the *Nightly News* anchor team make jokes about Rob having been brought up on the sidelines. Monday through Friday nobody paid any attention to him. On Jewish High Holidays he gave the economic report.

He followed Sonni to her desk. "So?" he asked.

"So what?" she snapped. She thumbed through her messages. Her father had phoned three times.

"Did you have a nice weekend?"

"Swell. Perfect. Wonderful. Terrific. Great, okay?"

"Was it that bad?"

"No, but I'm just not in the mood for—" She heard a loud crash across the hall. "What was that?"

"The workmen. They started today."

There were several resounding bangs and some shouts.

Sonni shook her head. "Oh, great. Just what I needed." She smacked her desk. "I don't see what's wrong with the way our offices are."

"No uniformity. Makes us look like a small network; big advertisers don't like small networks."

"Giving everyone Formica-topped desks, a Naugahyde armchair, and four trac lights is going to make us impressive?"

"Only the executives get four. Everyone else gets three. And no arms on the chair. It's supposed to promote corporate spirit while keeping employees in line."

"Why don't they just ask us to wear brown shirts?"

"Bring it up at the meeting, which, by the way, is in fifteen minutes." He headed for the door. "Oh, and I'd better warn you. You might get some flak from Albie about last week's assignments. Carla was not happy about covering that sewage backup on Long Island."

"That's tough—"

"Her sentiments exactly." He shrugged. "But you know Carla." He left.

Sonni did indeed know Carla. What Carla Lampretti liked best was to interview rape victims, police widows, and recently mugged senior citizens. Her idea of a dream story would have been the sack of Rome. Anything vaguely political or economic was "too establishment." She was, as she put it, "into compassion." She was also good at other things. As Albie Drury's secretary, Carla had discovered

the importance of working overtime—whenever Muffy
Drury was out at Fire Island. Carla acquired her journal-
ism experience through long hours on her boss's couch.
Her meteoric rise from secretary to action reporter surprised no one, except, possibly, Drury's wife, though it
was rumored that Muffy was having an affair with an
executive over at ABC and didn't give a damn.

Sonni glanced through the day's news stories, then
checked her watch. She had time for a quick call to her
father.

He picked up on the first ring.

"Mishkin Enterprises. Mishkin here to hear you." It was
his standard telephone salutation. Sonni had told him long
ago that it was corny and embarrassing, but he'd coun-
tered with "So is sex," and the matter was never brought
up again.

"Hi, Daddy. It's me."

"Son? Why, what an unexpected surprise."

"You called me three times."

"So I did." He hung up.

Sonni stared at the phone. Dear God, she hoped he
wasn't getting senile. She dialed again.

"Mishkin Enterprises. Mishkin here to—"

"Daddy, did you hang up?"

"Two," he said, and there was a click.

She quickly redialed.

"Mishkin Ent—"

"Daddy, what—?"

"*Now* we're even. If I'm going to talk man to man to
someone, I want to be on an equal footing."

"Dammit, Dad, will you stop that. I'm not someone.
I'm your daughter. A woman."

There was silence from the other end of the phone. Sonni knew that her father was lighting a cigar. "I just like to

think of you as my equal," he said, slightly miffed. "That's all."

"I don't need a penis for that."

"I was speaking figuratively. No need to get your balls in an uproar."

"Daddy!"

"It's just an expression. Boy, you're touchy. Maybe I should call back later."

"I'm going to be tied up all day." She looked at her watch. "In fact, I have a meeting in five minutes. If you have something to say, you'd better tell me now."

"You think I'd phone three times if I *didn't* have something to say?"

It was not beyond precedent. Very often Irv Mishkin would call just to ask the correct time, or if she could believe it took him two hours to find his glasses, which were on top of his head all along, or if she knew that some celebrity or other was Jewish. For him, small talk was high art.

"If it's about your Dinky, I don't—"

"Did I say Dinky?"

"No, but—"

"You disappoint me, Son. You never used to jump to conclusions."

"Every phone call I've gotten from you in the past month has been about that Dinky. Why should this one be different?"

"There's a big difference between what should be and what is. I was just calling to share some joy with you. I met a very special woman."

"Another one?" Irv Mishkin met only "very special" women. They were never nice, exciting, stimulating, or even pleasant. They were always "very special." Which could mean anything from outrageously rich to inconceivably ordinary. His fantasy was to have a beautiful woman dressed in black, whom nobody would know, attend his funeral. Two years ago his very special woman was a deaf meat-packing heiress who pressured him to learn sign language on the pretext of wanting him to teach her the lyrics of current rock tunes. As it turned out, she merely wanted him to learn enough to "talk" dirty to her in bed. "I didn't mind," Irv Mishkin had confided to his daughter in a bar after the affair broke up, "but then she criticized my foreplay! Hell, a man only has two hands!"

"Her name's Flossie," Irv Mishkin said. "A real go-getter. Cute as a button."

In addition to being very special, all her father's women were go-getters and cute as buttons; until he broke up with them, at which point they become floozies. "She sounds like all the others."

"She is. That's what's so wonderful," Irv Mishkin said. "She's my kind of woman. Only this time she's a redhead."

"I don't understand you. Most people hate to make the same mistakes, but you're making them a way of life. It's ridiculous."

"What's ridiculous? I'm a man who knows what he likes. Listen, Son, if there's one thing I've learned from the novelty business it's human nature. People always want something new; but no matter what they say, they like what they like. And as long as you give them the same thing in a different package, they'll buy it. TV is just radio in a different package. Variety might be the spice of life, but it's the same as oregano. It only works on things you like."

"I have to go," Sonni said.

"Flossie's coming over on Friday night to make spaghetti. How's about joining us?"

"I was thinking about going to the Hamptons."

"Nice place," Irv Mishkin said. "Just keep in mind that it'll be around when I'm not."

Sonni closed her eyes. "I'll be there around eight."

"Swell. Oh, and, Son . . ."

"Yes?"

"It's not going to be anything fancy, so don't bother stopping off for wine."

"Okay."

"But if you could remember the three thousand?"

She hung up the phone. *"Damn Yankees!"*

The meeting in Albie Drury's office was already under way when Sonni entered. She took a fresh cup of coffee from Albie's latest secretary, Tina, a wispy, blue-eyed black girl who had none of Carla's journalistic potential but who could type a hundred and eighty words a minute and rattle off obscure facts about Third World nations faster than an AP ticker. She knew more about Rwanda, Uganda, and Burundi than three-fourths of the UN Security Council. She was saving her money to open an exercise club in Bujumbura, where she had friends, relatives, and roots; where, she said, she was considered a black Jane Fonda.

Three of the station's management executives were there, which was unusual. They were rarely seen outside their offices by the WCBN news staff, except at Christmas, when they would follow Michelangelo, the mail room boy, and offer season's greetings as Michelangelo handed everyone a box of Fanny Farmer chocolates. Sonni recognized them only because she saw their photographs every day in the reception room. The photographs were hung on a wall between a plaque commemorating

WCBN's 1978 softball championship and their coverage
of New York's poop-scooping campaign.

Albie made perfunctory introductions, raising his voice
in order to be heard over the construction din. Sonni
smiled politely at Mr. De Lucca, Mr. Van Danner, and
Mr. Le Berman in turn. They dressed so similarly—gray
suits, blue shirts, and charcoal ties—that most of the staff
confused them. The way people kept them straight was by
remembering that Mr. De Lucca wore glasses, Mr. Van
Danner wore a hearing aid, and Mr. Le Berman was a
prick.

Sonni took a seat next to Ernie Hemmingway, the station's comptroller. Though his presence was not as surprising as that of De Lucca, Van Danner, and Le Berman, it
was equivalently unusual.

"Did I miss anything?" Sonni whispered.

"That depends," he said.

"Depends?"

"On whether you were aiming for something," he said,
examining his nails.

Odd, she thought. Though she barely knew him except
to say good morning or good night to in the elevator, that
wasn't a remark she would expect from Ernie Hemmingway. A short, taciturn fortyish bachelor, he was a serious
accountant who rarely left his office and never socialized
with the staff. Even when he smiled he looked depressed.
He suffered from his homonymous name. Bearing no re-
lation to the writer, and quick to point out that the other
Hemingway was spelled with one *m*, he was reputed to
gruffly admonish new staff members who often unwit-
tingly approached him with copy for clarification of syn-
tax. The fact that he was solidly built, with dark curly hair
well salted with silver, and bore a striking resemblance to

Norman Mailer compounded the problem, since many of the younger staff members often confused Ernest Hemingway with Norman Mailer anyway. Rob Carey had told Sonni that Hemmingway lived in the Village with a boa constrictor named Bruce, contributed recipes to the New York *Times* under a female pseudonym, and was a former Green Beret. Rob Carey made it his business to know everything he could about everyone at WCBN, quietly banking it with the hope that it would be negotiable if he were ever given the sack.

Sonni smiled uneasily at Ernie, then turned her attention to Albie, who ran his fingers through his hair theatrically as he spoke.

"I could mince words," he said somberly, which he couldn't, "but I won't. The *Nightly News* ratings are down, and it's up to us to do something about it. Last week we came out behind a rerun of an old Esther Williams clinker, and that was *with* Carla's special report on child molesters' victims."

"It would have been a better report if I hadn't been tied up on Long Island," Carla said, pointing the remark at Sonni.

"I don't invent the news," Sonni said sweetly, "I just assign it." She felt like asking Ernie if his boa constrictor would be up to a little foul play.

The carpenters' hammers began another jungle tattoo in the hall.

"Maybe that's the problem," Mr. De Lucca said, trying to make himself heard over the noise. "Speaking for management—" he looked from side to side at Mr. Le Berman's and Mr. Van Danner's nodding heads to assure himself that he was—"I think we've got to goose the show."

Albie Drury blanched. "Loose the show?"

"Goose it," Mr. De Lucca shouted.

"Give it a shot up the old kazoo," added Mr. Le Berman.

Albie looked relieved. At fifty-nine, the former producer of two unsuccessful game shows and publisher of a
short-lived Westchester newspaper knew that the *Nightly
News* was his last professional stand, and, as he had once
told Sonni, he wasn't about to let it go sitting down.

"I was just about to say that myself," he said. "What the
show needs is a shot up the old bazoo—"

"Kazoo," Mr. Le Berman corrected.

Albie leaned forward, straining to hear. "Whazoo?"

"Kazoo!" Mr. Le Berman shouted.

"Bless you," said Mr. Van Danner.

"Thank you," Albie said, and continued. "All right,
we've got to keep a few things in mind. Nothing succeeds
like success, and until we're successful we're not going to
make it. Mimicking the other networks isn't good enough.
We've got to innovate. I thought when we hired Marianna
that we were onto something, but the feedback we've gotten from her singing the weather report is bad. We have
to refill the spot with gold."

"Sounds like my dentist," Sonni muttered.

"Not another one like Lampell," Mr. De Lucca warned.
"That dressing-for-the-weather business was a disaster.
He looked like a goddam mugger in the ski mask."

"Ridiculous, of course," Albie agreed, flushing slightly.
Lampell's costumes had been his idea. "But, okay. That's
why we're here. Let's face it, the WR has always been a
good minority spot and we should keep it that way. But
why imitate other news shows? There are three minorities
that have never been touched—gays, senior citizens, and
the handicapped."

"No faggots," Mr. Le Berman said. He put his thumb
down to show he meant it.

"Old people smell weird," Mr. De Lucca said, wrinkling his nose while cleaning his glasses with his suit pocket, which he'd turned inside out. De Lucca was the youngest of WCBN's triumvirate. "No one wants to hear about a heat wave from someone who smells weird."

"My sentiments exactly," Albie said. "That's why I was thinking of a handicapped person."

"Cripples give me the creeps," Carla said. She wiggled her shoulders to demonstrate.

"I was thinking of a handsome, virile-looking paraplegic in a snazzy wheelchair," Albie said.

"Yeah," said Mr. De Lucca. "I can see that."

"Sounds good," said Mr. Van Danner.

"Gold," marveled Mr. Le Berman. "A weatherman in a wheelchair."

Sonni was appalled. She'd heard few things as repugnantly exploitive in her life and said so, only no one but Ernie Hemmingway heard her above the construction noise.

"Keep listening," he said. He didn't look at her when he spoke; his lips barely moved. It struck her that he might have been taught ventriloquism as a Green Beret, which he hadn't. He had been taught it, she learned sometime later, by his Uncle Phil, a former Borscht Belt entertainer turned Hollywood agent who had made his living talking from both sides of his mouth.

"I don't feel I can stomach it," Sonni said.

"You can stomach a lot more than you think you can, when it's your job." He sounded a lot like John Wayne and a little like her father, who'd taught her the Protestant work ethic even before right from wrong.

"From here on," Albie continued, shouting now, "slow news days are out. We can't afford 'em. We're in a show-business medium and we have to compete. I'm inaugurating a quota system, and the *Nightly News* is going to deliver a minimum of three crimes of passion, two diasters, and/or one cancer scare a night."

Sonni exploded. "That's ridiculous. How can you guarantee things like that? What if there are no disasters, no cancer scares?"

"Review old ones. Speculate on new ones. Hype whatever we have. Face it, we're a public service, and we have to give the public what they want. Remember, news doesn't just happen—it has to be made."

Sonni was in foul spirits when she left the office at noon. Lunch at the Four Seasons Grill was a treat, especially with Joanna and Karen, whom she'd known since college; but Albie Drury's quota system outraged her, the phone call to her father still distressed her, and the charley horse that knotted her thigh muscles tighter than wet bootlaces mercilessly reminded her of Wyatt Stelson.

She remained subdued as Joanna and Karen swapped gossipy morsels about mutual acquaintances in publishing and the film industry, those being their respective fields. Joanna Holbrook, at thirty-three, was the highly respected vice-president and editor in chief of a large paperback house. A severely attractive woman, slender to the point of medical concern, with faultless Nordic features and wheat-blond razor-cut hair, Joanna had a wardrobe whose annual cost was more than the average new home's and sported enough designer initials to construct a short novel. Joanna was *known* at the Four Seasons Grill. She lunched there regularly and enjoyed being assured "her table."

Joanna's table was in a line with other publishing executives' tables, but offered the best view of the restaurant's upper level, where the film executives had their tables. Karen Hass, who was the East Coast story editor for Sussex

Films, had *her* table on the upper level. When she and Joanna lunched together, they'd often argue about whose table they were going to sit at. When they lunched separately, they'd acknowledge each other with a small wave. Others in the restaurant would do the same to people they knew. Almost everyone in the Four Seasons Grill knew someone, so there was usually quite a bit of waving going on. Rarely did anyone with a standing table at the Four Seasons Grill look at a menu, preferring, as they did, to order their "usual" every day.

Karen and Joanna were almost through with their usuals (cold poached salmon, for one; poolroom chef's salad for the other; and occasionally vice versa) when they realized Sonni had hardly said a word.

"I just realized you've hardly said a word," said Joanna, adding that she'd actually realized it earlier, but hadn't wanted to say anything about it. She was known as one of the most closemouthed people in publishing.

"I don't feel very talkative," Sonni said.

"It's got to be your job, your father, or your sex life," Karen said sagely.

"All three."

"Start with your sex life. Is he married?"

"You would ask that," Sonni said, which was true. Karen's involvements with married men were as frequent and unsuccessful as her diets. Though not fat, she had a jovial roundness that denied her leotards, bikinis, jumpsuits, horizontal stripes, and desserts, but which was compensated for by a lavish mane of blue-black hair and firm breasts of seismic proportion. She also had a good sense of humor, which helped when her married men returned to their wives.

"She might not want to talk about it," Joanna said, attuned as she was to reticence.

"Of course she wants to," said Karen. "Don't you?"

"Well, to be truthful, no."

"Don't be so honest. Tell," urged Karen.

"Dammit. Not you too," Sonni said, suddenly feeling like Diogenes swinging a night-light in a black hole. She told them about the quota system and management's pushing for a paraplegic weatherman. "I mean, Jesus, it's a news show, not *Fantasy Island*. Drury already has the writers doctoring stories when he feels hard facts might upset viewers. Last week the market took the biggest nose dive of the year, and we reported it slightly off. On the other hand, an accidental trash-basket fire on Lexington Avenue was hyped so much it was ludicrous. I mean, it wasn't much more than a smoldering Marlboro, but we made it sound as if the PLO, the SLA, and the FALN had launched a combined terrorist attack on Bloomingdale's. If I didn't have to pay my rent, eat, buy clothes, or go anywhere, I'd quit."

"Sounds as if you're suffering from scruples," said Joanna.

"It's better than herpes," said Karen, who'd had her share of venereal ups and downs.

"Not by much," said Joanna, who'd never been afflicted with either. Joanna had bought *My Side*, the autobiography of Wilbur Casey, the homosexual child murderer, after six other publishers had turned it down. The book pandered to the emotionally disturbed, went through thirteen printings, established a genre of sick bios, and elevated Joanna to the vice-presidency of her company. "Scruples are the number-one killer for anyone in the media," she said.

"Screw scruples," Sonni said. "I'm talking about simple honesty, integrity."

"Doesn't sell books," Joanna said.

"Or movies."

"I've always hated the outrageous exaggerations my father's used to peddle his novelties. I swore I'd never go into that sort of business. And now I find that I'm in it. Nobody levels with anybody anymore," Sonni said, with a legitimate bitterness that surprised her, "about anything."

"Ah-ha," Karen said. "Now we're getting to it. You're sleeping with someone and he's a bastard."

"I slept with someone period. And he was a shit." Sonni took a sip of her drink as if to wash a bad taste from her mouth. "Would you believe he thought I was a hooker? He left me a hundred dollars."

"Well, at least he wasn't a cheap shit," Karen said.

"I wish I had a hundred dollars for every shit I've been to bed with," Joanna mused. Of all Sonni's friends, Joanna had the most active sex life. She was turned on by men in uniform and had done more for the morale of several precincts than the Police Benevolent Association ever could. She was also the only one of Sonni's friends who'd never had an orgasm. It gave her, she'd said, something to look forward to.

"A hundred dollars? Who wouldn't?" said Karen. "I could own an airline by now."

"It really upset me," Sonni said.

"Why? Think of all the times you went to bed with someone and didn't get paid—and felt you deserved to. God knows, I can," Karen said. "Do you remember Norman?"

"The Mormon?"

Karen nodded. "The same. Three wives, seven kids, and the only way he could stay sexually excited was to smell coffee brewing. Do you know what it's like to get

out of bed two, three, four times a night to put up coffee?
Never mind the cost, my house smelled like the inside of a
percolator. If I'd gotten three hundred bucks a night, I
think I'd still be underpaid."

"I feel miserable about the whole thing," Sonni said.

"Console yourself at Saks," Joanna suggested. "That's
what I'd do. And believe me, I'd have a terrific time doing
it. I wouldn't mind earning some money in my spare time
with a few tax-free lays, and, frankly, I can't think of
many single women who would—even a few married
ones, for that matter.

"Maybe I ought to start charging Larry," Karen said.
"It might eliminate his guilt and cut his therapist bills in
half."

"It would probably do that for a lot of guys," Joanna
said.

"I'll bet it would. An honest fuck for an honest buck,"
said Karen brightly, as if she'd just invented the world's
oldest profession.

Sonni laughed. "You make it sound like something
American males are suddenly ripe for; like an idea whose
time has—" She stopped. Thundering into her head came
the words that had been drummed into her since childhood, the words she'd accepted as a rune without meaning, no more meaning than "Hickory, Dickory, Dock."
She heard them now, clarion clear, in the same singsong
stentorian tone in which they'd always been spoken: *If
you find an idea whose time has come, the world is your
clamshell.*

It was time to take sex out of singles bars and put it on a
P-and-L ledger.

It was time to stop screwing around for free.

It was time for Sonni to claim her clamshell.

She thumped the table with her fist. "Let's order another drink," she said. "I have an idea that could eliminate a lot of guilt and make us a lot of money."

"See what talking about your sex life can do," Karen said. "You're in much better spirits."

"That I am," said Sonni.

She was happy as a clam.

Chapter 5

"For the last time," Sonni said, growing impatient with Karen's wisecracks, "I'm serious about this. If you're not interested, say so." By now the restaurant was almost empty.

"How could I not be interested?" Karen clasped her hands and sat up very straight. "Go on." She stifled a giggle.

"All right. Now, as I was saying, on a tactical level for men, call girls are emotionally cheaper than affairs, but practically speaking they're expensive and not all that easy to find. Also, guys don't need a Surgeon General's report to recognize that street hookers can be dangerous to their health. Basically they want *nice* girls; they want a change of scenery but not a surprise. That's why they sleep with women like us."

"That's not true," Karen said indignantly. "Norman loved me."

"Sure," Sonni said. "So why did he go back to his wife?"

"Well . . . he was honorable. That's what I liked about him."

"Come on," Sonni said. "Granting a few exceptions, most guys who take out a woman and go to bed with her either pretend to get involved or feel guilty about it. My feeling is, why not let them be up front, and why not let us make a profit at the same time? Honest business. Plain and simple."

"That's hooking!" Karen said, in a surprisingly uncharacteristic display of deduction.

"Well . . . I wouldn't call it *that*," said Sonni, who had already been mentally playing with the phrase "biological capitalism."

"But the cops would," Karen protested.

Joanna smiled and flicked the tip of her Gucci scarf across her lips. "Not the ones in my neighborhood," she said, adding modestly that she was practically an honorary member of the force.

"Then that's it," Sonni exclaimed. "We'll open up on your block."

"Oh, my God, you really *are* serious!" Karen grabbed Sonni's drink. "No more for you."

"It has potential," Joanna said, holding on to her glass. "If they ever legalize prostitution, we could be a 'Best Bet' in *New York* magazine."

"I don't believe you two. You want to open up a brothel on East Sixty-sixth Street. They wouldn't even give Richard Nixon a room there."

"It's a very good neighborhood," Joanna said.

"The only kind we should be in," said Sonni. "Besides, it's not as if we'll be hanging out a red light. We'll have some sort of respectable cover."

"Oh, right, sure." Karen nodded. "Who'd get suspicious about fifty men lining up in the hall every night for needlepoint instruction?"

"They won't be lining up in the hall," Sonni said, thinking as she spoke and speaking very slowly. "It will be done discreetly and by appointment. All we need is a plausible cover—something respectable that would conceivably bring a man out on a cold night to a woman's apartment."

Karen snorted and tossed her head. It was her standard derisive response. She'd copied it from Vivian Leigh in *Gone with the Wind*. Many of Karen's responses were culled from films. Imitating celebrated performers gave her a sense of security that none of her many therapists or lovers had been able to provide. The only trouble with her derisive head toss was that it was more equine than theatrical; more like Rhett's horse being ornery than Scarlett being cynical. "Lots of luck," she drawled.

Joanna said she couldn't think of anything besides sex that would bring a man out on a cold night, except perhaps his mother's cooking.

"A hot meal." Sonni snapped her fingers. "That's it!"

The waiter, who looked more like a hotel bellhop and was actually a woman in an androgynous gray-and-red uniform and cap, heard the snap and hurried to the table.

Sonni waved her away. "We're fine," she said.

The waitress looked piqued. Joanna asked her for the check to be polite, to be sure her table wouldn't be given to a Bantam or Random House editor tomorrow.

"It's perfect," Sonni said. "A cooking school. They have them in people's apartments all over the city. We could call it What's Cooking. It would be totally respectable."

"But not totally honest," said Karen, waving an incriminating finger like Margaret Rutherford's Miss Marple.

"Who says? We'll teach them to cook, too. It'll be an added attraction."

Joanna said that all she could make was a phone call to a caterer, but added that she used to be good at omelettes.

"Then we'll stick to omelettes," said Sonni. "Some butter, milk, eggs, and an apartment and we've got it made. It's a million-dollar idea."

"It's madness," said Karen, grinning now. "We could never get away with it."

"Of course we can," said Sonni. "Whoever heard of a raid on a cooking class? Julia Child used to have them at her place all the time."

"That was different," said Karen.

"Why?"

"Julia Child didn't put out."

That night the three friends got together at Sonni's apartment. Over a bottle of expensive champagne that came from a province in France where women were known for their omelettes and sexual favors, they agreed that what American men were ready for was a good, moderately priced lay.

"The really experienced call girls are getting five hundred a night," said Joanna. She had recently published Xaviera Hollander's final book, a view from retirement called *Silent Springs*, and knew a lot about the problems of the business.

"They deserve it," said Karen. "Look what they have to put up with."

"Oh, come on," Joanna protested, "we've all put up with less than rapture at one time or another."

"I'm talking about the weirdos, the ones who want to be diapered or tap-danced on."

"That's not our market," Sonni said. She made a note on the yellow legal pad she held on her lap. "We'll charge an even hundred. We're offering a dependable commodity and a service—sort of like a fast-food chain—for the average randy guy."

"But no take-out orders," cautioned Joanna. "That's where we could get in trouble."

Sonni agreed. "They won't mind, because they'll be getting reliable variety at an affordable price."

Karen wrinkled her nose and cocked her head, a coy manifestation of confusion she'd adapted from old Doris Day movies. "Reliable variety? Sounds like a cereal combination pack."

"We have to have a limited menu to be efficient," Sonni said, making another note on her pad. "It will work out best for everyone. What a guy orders, he gets. No surprises, no complaints. Our providers know what they're giving—and our customers know what they're getting. If someone wants, let's say, a number three, a number three it is."

Karen leaned over to look at Sonni's pad. "Did I miss something? What's a number three?"

"I don't know yet. That's where market research comes in. We have to nail down the most popular practices, time them for feasibility, and standardize them."

"Standardize!" Karen said. "How can you standardize sex?"

"The same way you standardize anything," Sonni said. "The way Mr. McDonald standardized the Big Mac."

"I hope I'm not the first to tell you," Karen said, "but there's a difference between a hamburger and a blow job."

Sonni leafed through her yellow pad after Joanna and Karen left. Admittedly there were a few details that needed ironing out. They had to find a large enough apartment, which could prove difficult, though Joanna had said she might have a line on a possibility. Nonetheless, Sonni would start going over the real-estate ads herself tomorrow. Her commitment was as clear as it was unshakable. On an ethical level, she was unencumbered by conscience. Just because sex was natural didn't mean it had to be free. Water was natural, and a lot of people paid for that. If a woman could make an honest living by giving men haircuts, what was less honest about giving them head?

When you came right down to it, it was just a ball game.

Lying in bed, she thought about all the women who at that very moment were playing for free, unaware that they could be paying their gas bill at the same time. It suddenly seemed to Sonni an incredible injustice. She felt for the first time since her sophomore year at Barnard that John Locke's *Essay Concerning Human Understanding* was more than just an excessive amount of homework; felt an empathy for Cesar Chavez.

She felt that she had found her niche.

Like Evita, Indira, Golda, Mother Teresa, she was at last a woman with a calling; a woman who had come to a crossroad and, without stopping to ask directions, had made the right choice.

She hadn't felt this way since the day she'd hung up her boxing gloves and relinquished her title to Harvey Glazer; that day had been the day after the day she'd ruined her reputation trying to preserve her honor by deviating Benny Shemski's septum with a right hook.

Benny Shemski was the most popular boy in the neighborhood, and the dullest. His remarkable lack of wit, intellect, and good looks was compensated for by his father's movie theater on Flatbush Avenue, where those chosen by The Shem could sit in the adult section and see the latest features for free. At fourteen Benny had felt up more girls than his nineteen-year-old cousin Arnold, who looked like James Dean, was captain of the football team, and the best dancer in Flatbush.

That day on Coney Island's Bay 8 beach, The Shem had sauntered over to the blanket where Sonni and her friends Marge and Lois were sitting and announced that he was going to interview them to see whom he'd invite to Sunday's show. He took Marge under the boardwalk for her interview first. When she returned, she said that all he did was ask some dumb questions about history that any idiot could answer. Lois went next and returned to say that he asked her dumb questions, too.

When Sonni got under the boardwalk, The Shem was leaning against a stanchion, smoking a Camel.

"I'm here for the interview," she said.

"Who discovered America?"

"Christopher Columbus."

"Who was the first President of the United States?"

"George Washington."

"Okay. It's a tie. Show me your tits."

Sonni was too stunned to move.

"Come on, come on," he said. "It's a Rock Hudson movie, and the popcorn's free."

He took a step toward her and she broke his nose.

The following day, his eyes black and his nose taped, he took Marge and Lois to his father's theater and spread the word that Sonni was a tramp. Harvey Glazer, who sparred with Sonni on Tuesday and Thursday afternoons, was enraged by the allegation and in the middle of "Coming Attractions" decked The Shem.

The punch kept The Shem out of school for a week and got Harvey banned from the theater for life.

When Sonni learned what had happened, she gave Harvey her title and hung up her gloves. Harvey went on to professional boxing, and later opened a gym in Lodi, New Jersey, where, Sonni had heard, one of Mohammed Ali's cousins trained.

The Shem never spoke to Sonni again. Marge and Lois did. They told her that they owed her an apology, that they had really wanted to see Rock Hudson; that they'd both shown Benny Shemski their tits.

Sonni wondered what Marge and Lois were doing now. She wondered if they knew how to make omelettes.

Chapter 6

Sonni awoke ravenous, but, having forgotten to set her alarm, she had barely enough time to grab a handful of Wheaties on her way out.

She never forgot her Wheaties.

When she was growing up, her father would leave the box on the table every night so that she couldn't miss them in the morning. Irv Mishkin believed in them the way some people did vitamins or God. He attributed everything, from his perfect prostate to his success with Glitter Marbles, to the Breakfast of Champions. Convinced that the only way his daughter could compete in a man's world was to think like a man, and that the first way to think like one was to eat like one, he made Sonni promise she'd never forget her Wheaties. Anytime she received a good grade or won a prize, he credited Wheaties. When, for a short period in her teens, she rebelled and said that she wanted to eat breakfast at the local doughnut shop, Irv Mishkin had her poll the poorest students in school to find out their diet.

None of them ate Wheaties. Irv Mishkin felt his point had been made. So did Sonni.

On mornings when her father had time, he also made her steak with fried eggs. She'd long ago given up the steak and eggs, but, as with all rituals that grow more powerful with time, nothing short of divine edict or a severe intestinal virus could force her to face the world without munching down at least a fistful of the champions' toasted flakes.

Two workmen were installing the last of three trac lights when she entered her office. The workmen were standing on her desk, several papers scrunched beneath their boots.

"Excuse me," Sonni said, poking the shorter one in the leg, "but you're stepping on my mail."

He lifted his foot. "Sorry, but we're not allowed to touch anything on the desks. Union rules."

Sonni snatched what she could before he lowered his foot. "That's ridiculous. What about ladders? Are they against the rules, too?"

"What do I look like, the answer man? Call Local 322 and ask, if you're that curious. We're just doing our job."

"Well, you don't have to be nasty about it," Sonni said.

"I think she's coming on to you, Frank," the taller one said.

Frank laughed. Sonni didn't. She gave them an icy look and sat down on her new Naugahyde chair to look through the mail. On top, interestingly embossed by the soles of the men's boots, was a memo to the WCBN staff from De Lucca, Van Danner, and Le Berman. The subject was office décor. Listed were four rules. The first prohibited any picture on the wall other than the company-issued Norman Rockwell lithograph which, it was noted, would be arriving in a week and was to be hung forty-eight inches from the floor. The second banned live plants, any books not required for the performance of duties, and personal photographs, with the exception of framed three-by-five snapshots of spouse, children, or aging parents; and those could be kept only on the left-hand side of the desk. The third forbade the exhibition of personal items, such as favorite *New Yorker* cartoons or birthday greetings. The fourth and last specified that no ashtrays other than WCBN's green ovals were allowed.

At the bottom, all in caps, was: "WE'RE BUILDING AN IMAGE—DON'T DISTORT IT."

Sonni shuddered at the image and tossed the memo into the wastebasket as the phone rang. She had to reach between the workmen's legs to answer it. The taller one mumbled something and gave a dirty laugh. She pretended not to notice.

Tina, Albie Drury's secretary, was calling to inform Sonni that Albie wanted her to handle the weatherperson interviews on Friday.

"Jesus," Sonni said. "What do I know about the weather?"

"It's supposed to be clear and warmer for the weekend."

Sonni realized it was pointless to press the issue.

"My cousin, George Wilkins, is going to apply," Tina said. "He knows his stuff. He was the first dude to get a bead on Hurricane David."

"Sounds good," Sonni said. "Um, what's—what's wrong with him?"

Tina sounded offended. "Nothin'."

"I mean," said Sonni, "we're supposed to get someone in a wheelchair."

"Hell, he'll sit in a wheelchair."

"Well, it's not that," Sonni said pleasantly, not wanting to alienate Tina. "Upstairs wants someone . . . handicapped."

"Oh, no problem," Tina assured her. "He's missing most of his toes. Lost them horsing around on a forklift. He's got a great sense of humor."

"I don't know," Sonni said. "I think they want someone who's *really* handicapped."

"You don't call a six-foot-two black man without toes handicapped?"

"Well . . ."

"He can't boogie, he can't play basketball—that's not handicapped?"

"I didn't say that—"

"Just because someone's not wheeled around and fed doesn't mean they're not handicapped in this male-dominated white middle-class society," she said icily. "Think about it."

Sonni said she would and hung up. She sighed and shook her head. It wasn't easy starting the day arguing with a black Jane Fonda on only a handful of Wheaties.

The men stepped down from the desk and prepared to leave. Frank tested the switch. "Aw-riiight!" he said.

"Thank you," Sonni said coolly. She began straightening up.

"Don't mention it," Frank said. "I could turn on for you all day long."

"If you'll excuse me," Sonni said, "there are some things I'd like to get done."

"There are some things *I'd* like to get *done*," Frank said, winking at his partner. They snickered and left.

Sonni slammed the door. The thought that creeps like that got it for free was intolerable. They shouldn't even be allowed in the ball park, which reminded her to check the real-estate section for an apartment that could be used for the school.

The next day Joanna called Sonni at the office. "Pay dirt!" she said. "I think I've found us a nest."

"No! Really?"

"Don't be so negative. Yes, really. How do eight rooms on East Seventy-second sound to you?"

"Expensive," Sonni said.

"Christ, you sound like my father." Joanna's father was an eccentric retired businessman who lived in terror of having to touch his capital; who lived in a trailer in Fort Lauderdale with a cat, a black-and-white TV, and a seventy-thousand-dollar ticker tape.

"I'm sorry," Sonni said. "I'm just excited. Tell me more."

"It's the perfect location. I went to a party there once. The owner is Pandy Palmetto, the rock star's widow. She's sort of a friend of a friend of mine who fixed some plumbing for her jacuzzi."

"Aha," said Sonni, "the wrench connection."

Joanna didn't laugh, which struck Sonni as usual for someone who didn't have orgasms.

"Anyway," Joanna continued, "Pandy's recently become a disciple of some guru, and she's following him to Jaipur. She's giving up her Laszlo membership, her Porsche, and subletting her apartment for two years."

"What happens after two years?" Sonni asked.

"She hopes to find true inner peace or another husband."

"Wonderful."

"And you haven't heard the best part."

"What's that?"

"The maintenance would only be about twenty guys a month."

"Fantastic," Sonni said. "Karen could probably cover that on her own. What about a security payment?"

"As much as we want to give her. Pandy said she's not into money as long as the vibes are right. The hitch is that we have to keep the place pretty much like it is—which might be a problem."

"Why?"

"The furnishings are a little offbeat."

"How far off?" asked Sonni warily. Joanna's idea of conservative was to the left of Salvador Dali. She'd had her apartment decorated by a SoHo conceptual artist who believed that objects should transcend function. Joanna's kitchen table was a former door, her bed a converted armoire. Her bathtub, one of the few things in the apartment that sort of was what it was, had once been a water trough for some New Jersey Guernseys.

"Well," said Joanna, "Pandy's husband was a sports nut. The place is loaded with baseball paraphernalia."

Sonni felt giddy. If ever there was a portent, this was *it*. It was too extraordinary to be coincidence. Sonni now felt certain that God was on her side, that even He was aware of the inequities of intercourse and had appointed her His arbitrator. "It's perfect," she said. "Tell her we'll be there tomorrow."

Sonni found it difficult to concentrate on the day's assignments, and inadvertently gave Carla Lampretti the

wrong background sheet for an interview. Carla was half-
way through her interview with a Queens librarian who
had been raped—and who persisted in saying, rapturous-
ly, that it was the greatest thing that had ever happened in
her life—before she realized a mix-up, discovered that
this was a Queens housewife who had just won the lottery.
Carla accused Sonni of deliberately humiliating her; Sonni pacified her by sending her out to Brooklyn to cover an
exceptionally bloody murder. Live.

By the time Sonni left the office, she was beat, and said
so to Ernie Hemmingway, whom she met in the elevator.

"I know the feeling," he said. "Days like this could
make a guy homesick for Nam." It was a very Mailer-
esque thing for Hemmingway to say.

They reached the street. He asked her if she wanted a
lift downtown, but he did it without moving his lips and in
such a fashion that Sonni looked behind her to see who
had spoken. When she turned back, Hemmingway was
gone. She shrugged, pushed the incident from her mind,
and didn't think of it until it happened again, which was
sometime later.

The following morning Sonni awoke before her alarm.
She was excited, as excited as she'd been when she discovered her first pubic hair—once again a new phase of her
life was beginning. The apartment was the first step on
the path that destiny had designed for her.

This was a morning for the Breakfast of Champions.

With a cry that sounded somewhere between a wolf
howl and an orgasmic release, she raised the box of Wheaties heavenward—a Viking toast to the gods—and acci-
dentally spilled the entire contents. She refused to think of
it as any sort of omen. Scooping what flakes she could into

a bowl, she added milk and brought her breakfast out to the living room. She turned on the TV and sat down. Before she put the spoon into her mouth she nearly choked.

On the screen, bewigged as the People's Person and looking rivetingly handsome, was Wyatt Stelson. He was staring into the camera and shouting at America's housewives.

"You're getting ripped off on plastic wrap and aluminum foil and don't even know it," he warned. "Why? Because there are no instructions on the boxes, because the manufacturers don't tell you what to do when your roll tears unevenly. Because that way you're forced to *buy more!* But that's unfair, you say. Deceitful. What do manufacturers care about honesty? I estimate that the average housewife, over the course of an average marriage—let's say five years—wastes enough convenience wrap trying to even out rolls to cover the entire state of Vermont!"

"Well!" the host of the show said, wiping his forehead as if Wyatt had just accused the President of child-molesting, "I'll bet we have a lot of viewers who have something they'd like to say about *that*." A phone number flashed on the screen. "The number is six, six, one, two, two, one, one, for all of you who want to speak out."

"I'll speak out," Sonni growled. She thrust her fist at the set and spilled her Wheaties on the couch. Cursing, she cleaned up the soggy flakes, which lay like dead wet moths upon the cushions.

The TV host repeated the phone number. Sonni wrote it down.

Wyatt was listening to a woman from Maplewood, New Jersey, tell a tale of woe about trying to wrap a Christmas turkey in foil only to wind up with strips no wider than tinsel. He nodded knowingly, sympathetically. Smugly. It

was the smugness that got to Sonni. She picked up the
phone and dialed. She was put on hold.

She waited and wondered what name she could use that
would conceal her identity from viewers yet still reveal it
to Wyatt. She came up with Ona Buss and Portia Author-
ity, neither of which she liked, and decided to use Ada
Miplace. She placed the hem of her nightgown over the
mouthpiece to disguise her voice. She wanted to humiliate
the sonofabitch in such a way that he would know it was
she, but be unable to prove it. She knew what she was
going to say. She was going to throw the bastard a curve
he couldn't handle. She was going to ask him why someone who was so dedicated to honesty wore a wig!

She heard a click; her pulse quickened. Should she bait
him or just sock it to him? The former, she decided, would
provide more embarrassment. Her opening remark was
on the tip of her tongue when the voice at the other end
informed her that they wouldn't have time to take her
call.

She slammed down the phone, sending two Picasso
prints crashing to the floor, which was still sticky from the
milk and Wheaties. It took her half an hour to clean up
the room—but less than a minute to vow eternal hatred
for a man she barely knew.

Sonni was late meeting Joanna and Karen, and apologized without giving details as they took the elevator up to
Pandy Palmetto's apartment. Pandy introduced herself as
Ta'Shi. She had taken the name in preparation for her trip
to Jaipur. Guru Baktawanda, she explained, had informed
her that *pandi* was Hindu slang for "vagina," and, as she
put it, she didn't feel she could hack a bunch of foreigners
calling her "Cunt" from the moment she arrived.

"It's the kind of thing that can bum you right out," she

said. She wore a deep-green robe over green satin tap shorts. While green wasn't her color, she said, it was the color of reality, and all Guru Baktawanda's disciples wore it.

"Sometimes," she said wistfully, "I wish reality was magenta. It would go so well with my hair."

Joanna, who had good color sense and equivalent tact, agreed.

Pandy showed them around the apartment, which was spacious and an incongruous blend of East and West, of Jaipur and jock—with a noticeable absence of rock. She explained that after Boo-Boo's demise she'd given away all of his records because it hurt too much to listen, and had kept only a small part of his sound system for old times' sake.

"He never even got to see 'Guyana Koolaid' go platinum," she sighed, taking them into the kitchen. Hanging from ceiling hooks, between copper pots, was a variety of baseball bats. "I couldn't bear to get rid of these. Music was his life, but baseball meant so much to him."

"I understand completely," Sonni said. Karen gave her a funny look.

The four bedrooms, which Ta'Shi told them Boo-Boo liked to keep available for his strung-out friends, were all Eastern in décor and contained the same framed eight-by-ten glossy. It showed Boo-Boo, his long straggly cream-colored hair parted in the center and falling in two clumps like Afghan hound ears past his shoulders, with his arm around Reggie Jackson. Each room also contained some piece of athletic equipment. A floor-mounted Exercycle was in one, a set of parallel bars in another, a third had a variety of weights and barbells, and the last a punching bag.

Boo-Boo Palmetto had had a phobia about growing old and flabby, a phobia that disintegrated along with his Learjet somewhere over New Mexico. Ta'Shi said that the Aeronautics Board had called it pilot error, but that Guru Baktawanda had said it was just Boo-Boo's karma.

"It's funny, though," she said, "that Boo-Boo's karma was the same as his backup singer's, his drummer's, his lead guitarist's, and his manager's. Group karma, I guess."

"It must be hard for you without him," Karen said, knowing what it felt like to lose husbands even if they did belong to other people.

"I used to miss him a lot," Ta'Shi said, "but since I got into celibacy I hardly even think about him. Like Guru Baktawanda says, you don't miss clothes if you're a nudist."

"He has a point," said Karen, who couldn't fathom it.

The living room was large enough to hold a small get-together for the Yankees and the Red Sox. Two long benchlike couches, covered in bright madras, faced each other from opposite sides of the room. Between them were four oversized Indian floor pillows set out in a diamond pattern. Boo-Boo Palmetto's baseball-card collection was framed in heavy oak above the fireplace. About the room, on the bookcase and the tables, interspersed between delicate incense burners, were more bats, and several mitts and a catcher's mask. Sonni found the place incredibly erotic.

Ta'Shi went to the kitchen to prepare some tea.

"Well," Joanna said. "what do you think?"

"I think it's great," Sonni said.

"Are you kidding?" Karen said. "With all this stuff? It looks like the New Delhi YMCA." Karen was an ardent

Minimalist. What few furnishings she had in her apartment were as white as the walls and ceiling; her visitors often had the odd sensation of entering an igloo.

"I don't think we should change a thing," Sonni said. "All we need are a few homey . . . sort of single-girlish touches—an avocado plant, a cat, a litter box in the bathroom, maybe a couple of framed prints, some cute magnets on the refrigerator. It'll be perfect. There'll be just enough yin to make men romantic and just enough yang to make them comfortable."

"And enough fucking baseball bats to make a log cabin," said Karen. "How are we going to cook in there without getting concussions?"

"We'll work around them." Sonni liked the kitchen bats. Alongside the copper pots, she thought, they were discreetly phallic.

Ta'Shi returned with the tea, which was green and tasted like liquid parsley, which, she informed them, it was.

"Parsley is an herb of truth, a symbol of eternal honesty," she said. "Our drinking it together is a contract."

"It's very good," said Sonni, swallowing with difficulty, acutely aware that in behalf of honest sex she was lying through her teeth.

Chapter 7

During the next few weeks Sonni thought only about two things: honest sex and her father. The former caused her to lose weight, run her phone bill up well over a hundred dollars, and buy eight-millimeter copies of films that just a year before she had joined in a demonstration to ban. The latter caused her migraines.

The migraines began the Friday night she'd planned to give her father the three thousand for his Dinky; the night she went to his apartment for dinner and found him helping a half-naked fifty-six-year-old woman make shrimp chowder and spaghetti.

"Son. What a pleasant surprise!" Irv Mishkin said, throwing an arm around her shoulders. Her father's expressions of affection had always been more fraternal

than paternal. Just before her marriage to Lenny, Irv
Mishkin took her out to Steak and Brew with his friends,
who got drunk and told stories about cheating on their
wives with waitresses in places like Bayonne and Paramus.
Afterward they all went to a club in the Village where
there were topless go-go dancers. She was the only girl she
knew who'd been given a bachelor party instead of a
shower.

"You called twice today to remind me to come," Sonni
reminded him, glancing uneasily at the redheaded woman, who was stirring a pot on Irv Mishkin's stove. She wore
lime-green slacks and a pink brassiere; a cigarette dangled
from the corner of her mouth. She looked like someone
from a Fellini outtake. What was even more disturbing,
she looked familiar.

"Of course I called," Irv said. "Who knows better than
your father how executives can forget things?"

"I'm not an executive yet."

"Don't cry to me, talk to your boss. Come on." He led
her toward the kitchen. "I want you to meet my guest."

"Guest my ass." The woman laughed, flashing caps the
size of Mah-Jongg tiles. "I've been cooking since five, and
shvitzing enough to make another pot of soup, which is
nothing compared to when I made kugel for twenty in
California and it was a hundred and seven degrees outside
and in. Now *that* was cooking, believe me." She wiped
her hand on a dish towel. "I'm a little wet, but I'm still
Flossie Gerber."

"Nice to meet you," Sonni said.

They shook hands and Sonni averted her eyes from the
mounds of dappled flesh that rose above the cups of the
pink brassiere, which was already stretched to a frighten-
ing measure. Sonni marveled at the endurance of latex.

"I hope you don't mind the informality," Flossie said.

"Emily Post might not approve, but *I* was hot as hell, and"—she winked—"your father didn't seem to mind."

"What did I tell you?" Irv Mishkin nudged Sonni with his elbow. "Something, eh?"

Flossie pinched Irv's cheek, pulling his face toward hers. "*You're* something," she said huskily. "Your father is one of a kind," she told Sonni.

"I know," Sonni said.

"What do you know?" You're just a kid. *I* know. My last husband died some time ago, and until I saw this face"— she pinched Irv's cheek again—"I couldn't even look at another guy. I'm not letting *this* one get away. I'll tell you, kiddo, your dad is *quite* a man."

The implication was palpable. Irv Mishkin turned as pink as Flossie's brassiere. Sonni felt a headache tuning up. It wasn't the innuendo that bothered her. She knew more about her father's sex life than most women knew about their husbands'. He had always been as candid with her about his bedroom habits as he was about his business.

Irv Mishkin firmly believed that the more his daughter knew about the other side, the better she'd be able to succeed on her own. He'd taught her about wet dreams before he explained menstruation; taught her that the average penis was six inches, and the average intercourse was seven minutes, and that no matter what anyone told her to the contrary, semen would do absolutely nothing for her complexion. He confided lines he used to seduce women and the maneuvers he employed to excite them, tendered dispassionate, virtually academic reports on his physical and emotional responses to how they performed in bed. He supplemented her education with the *Playboy* "Advisor" column and tapes he'd recorded in the men's locker room of the Ninety-second Street Y.

No, what bothered Sonni about Flossie's remark was not that it smacked of sex—it reeked of marriage.

Sonni was in favor of her father remarrying. She had lobbied for it several times over the years, but the women she liked were never the ones he did. He needed, he said, a very special woman. Flossie Gerber was special, all right. So were the Bacchae—which didn't mean one had to like them. Sonni was surprised by her instant antagonism, but there was something ominous about the woman. Maybe it was her *I*'s—*I* know, *I* am. Maybe it was her pink brassiere.

"All right, you guys, out of my kitchen." Flossie kissed the bald dome of Irv Mishkin's head. "Why don't you make your kid a drink and refill my bourbon while you're at it, huh, Irvala?"

Irvala? Sonni stiffened.

Her father melted. He gave Flossie an affectionate pat and led Sonni back into the living room. "Something, eh?" he said.

"Something," said Sonni, not sure of what.

Over drinks her father told Sonni that Flossie was certain his Dinky was a surefire successor to the Hula-Hoop and that she was willing to help him market it. She was, Irv said, a shrewd businesswoman who knew her stuff, which was, by amazing coincidence, novelties.

"She's the mother of the talking toilet seat," he said, with no mean admiration. "Unfortunately someone else beat her to the Patent Office, but she has lemonade glasses ready to go." Said glasses were water tumblers permanently coated with lemon flavor. "When you add water, you have instant, no-calorie lemonade. She's thinking of making them in other flavors too, once the lemon starts selling. All she needs is a lucky break and a few thousand dollars."

"Where's she going to get the money?" Sonni asked, suspecting that Flossie was already in the process of arranging her lucky break.

"Well, I thought that maybe you could sort of loan . . ."

Sonni gaped. "You're talking about *Mother's* money."

"She loved lemonade."

Flossie singsonged from the kitchen, "Hold onto your tummies, it's coming in a minute."

"Never," Sonni said, unconsciously gripping her purse tighter. "Why doesn't she go to a bank?"

"They don't give loans for lemonade."

"Soup's on!" Flossie placed a large tureen on the table. She hooked her thumbs under her bra straps and looked pleased.

"It smells wonderful," Irv said.

"Wonderful? It smells marvelous." She faced Sonni. "What do you say?"

"I'm sure it's terrific."

"Terrific? It's *fabulous*. But how about that aroma, huh?"

"Well, to be honest, I can't really tell. I have occasional sinus problems and—"

"You think *you* have sinus problems? Four years ago mine were so blocked up I thought there was cement in there. And the pain, my God!"

"It can be severe."

"You don't know the half of it. They gave me enough codeine and Demerol to relax Mount Saint Helens and I was still in agony. My doctor—let me tell you, the *best* in the field—even *he* said he'd never seen anything like it. I drained for two days."

"It must have been awful," Irv said.

"It was worse! Well—" Flossie smacked her thighs—"I

guess I should dress for dinner, huh?" She left without waiting for an answer.

"You see why I say she's special? Look," Irv Mishkin whispered, "if she had access to funds and I needed, they'd be mine like a shot. She's a carer, a giver."

Flossie reentered, tugging down a T-shirt on which was written "What's Mine Is Yours." Irv poked his daughter as if to say, "What-did-I-tell-you?"

Sonni stared. It was the T-shirt that did it—the same T-shirt that she, Flossie, had worn on the Trailways bus last Sunday. A carer? A giver? The woman was a taker from the word *mine*.

Sonni couldn't eat, but neither her father nor Flossie noticed. Irv was busy concentrating on Flossie—repeatedly calling her his Gerber Baby—and Flossie was busily pouring out her marital saga without omitting a drop.

"My first marriage was the biggest mistake anyone could make," she said, taking a hefty forkful of spaghetti.

"Don't be so hard on yourself," Irv said. "Lots of people make mistakes the first time around. Right, Son?"

Sonni nodded reluctantly.

"Not like mine, oh no. Two people were *never* more unsuited for each other. Nancy Reagan and Idi Amin would have made a better couple."

"Anyone can have bad luck," Irv said sympathetically. "Look at those actresses in Hollywood."

"Oh, yeah? How many do you know whose marriages ended on their wedding night?"

Irv gaped. "On your wedding night?"

"He came out of the bathroom wearing my negligee."

"*Veyizmier!*"

"I knew right then it wasn't a match made in heaven,

but what was worse, he had his *own* packed in his suitcase!" She took a gulp of water. "My second marriage—well, you could call it incompatibility, but, as far as I'm concerned, it was just bad timing; Phil was never ready when I was. But then . . . then there was Mel."

Sonni looked up. The roster was growing impressively. "Mel?"

"My last husband. He would have been perfect if he hadn't gambled, drunk and played the bassoon. God, that's an awful instrument. Did you ever hear it? What pleasure someone could take in an instrument that sounds like a whale with heartburn is still beyond me."

"Is that why you divorced him?" Sonni asked.

"I never divorced him. He was hit by a bus." Flossie sighed. "One minute he was there—the next, he was grill-work."

"How terrible," Sonni said.

"I'll tell you *how* terrible. His brother was driving the bus."

"No!" Irv said.

"Oh, yes. And what was even more terrible, I was riding in it at the time—"

"No!"

"And his mother was sitting next to me."

"Good God," Sonni murmured.

"That you survived all that is incredible," said Irv. "And without a nervous breakdown? A miracle."

"You're telling *me*? I probably couldn't have gone on if it weren't for my son, Seymour." Seymour was a California nutritionist who believed that the right vitamins could cure everything from the blues to the clap; a natural-food activist who credited the option to decline MSG in Chinese food as one of the most significant advances in healthy gastronomy since wheat germ. She stressed that

Seymour had values other than money, that while he supported her emotionally and nutritionally, he was no help at all financially. She told Irv he was lucky to have a daughter like Sonni, then let her voice trail off.

Sonni sensed the direction the conversation was taking and decided it was time to leave.

"So early?" Irv asked, surprised.

"I have an awful headache."

"I used to have migraines so bad they had to shoot me up with morphine," Flossie said. "Once I was hospitalized for a week."

Irv Mishkin massaged his temples. He was prone to empathetic physical reactions. When Sonni had had appendicitis, his palm never left his side. Just reading articles on vasectomies could send him doubling over as if he'd been kicked in the groin.

"Well, we didn't get to talk much about the Dinky," he said, "but Flossie thinks it's ready and so do I."

"That's great."

"So? Can I expect a check?"

Sonni had been prepared to give him the money that night, to surprise him, but with Flossie right there it would almost be like handing a kid a hamburger in the presence of a lion.

"You can expect a check," she said.

"Soon?"

"Soon."

She could have sworn she heard Flossie growl.

In the weeks that followed, rarely a day passed without some dunning from her father. He even took to sending postcards: "Haven't you forgotten something?" It wasn't like him. Oh, he had nagged before, but he'd never waged a campaign. Flossie had to be behind it.

Sonni had tried to erase her first impression of Flossie, but it was like trying to erase Hiroshima or Watergate. Some things were indelible. Even overlooking the woman's obvious designs on Irv—and in all probability his Dinky as well—her rampant upsmanship annihilated whatever latent amicable feelings Sonni might have been able to muster. If Irv was tired, Flossie was exhausted. If he was happy, she was euphoric. No matter how wonderful anyone's experience, hers was better; no matter how awful, hers was worse. It was infuriating enough to tempt Sonni to fake suicide just to see how far Flossie would go to best her.

Sonni finally sent a check in the hope that her father would become so involved with the Dinky that he'd lose interest in his Gerber Baby. The faster he broke from her, the better off he'd be. Sonni knew this, but she wished she didn't. Knowing what was best for her father distracted her from determining what would be pleasurable for other men—which was essential if she intended to turn a simple American pastime into big business.

Sex in theory was much more complicated than it was in bed. Sonni discovered this after two weeks of sitting down with Joanna, Karen, a calculator, and a stopwatch trying to reduce the myriad permutations of heterosexual activity to three standard couplings, a single oral sex act, and one quickie manual tension reliever.

While in some ways it had been much easier than she'd thought, in others it was far more difficult than she could have imagined. Joanna and Karen had elected her "First Madam," explaining that since she'd created the school, she deserved to manage it. It was a flattering vote of confidence, but it was also a cop-out. It left Sonni the brunt of the work.

Not that she minded; working was her second nature.

Her father's single ecumenical concession had been to teach her the Protestant Ethic. When she was a child, he'd sat on her bed nightly and inculcated her with stories about diligent tortoises, tenacious rodents, and persevering locomotives. As she grew older, he forced the Horatio Alger books upon her, the *Ragged Dick* series and *Luck and Pluck*. Work became as natural and unshakable a part of her life as eating Wheaties. She worked at making friends, worked at Woolworth's; when there were problems, she worked them out; when there were things to be done, she worked them in. She worked over people and worked under them. Sometimes she even worked at having fun. The only thing she'd never worked at, never had to work at, was sex. And now she was even working at that.

For five solid nights, she, Joanna, and Karen had sat through reel after reel of eight-millimeter porn films, and, at Sonni's insistence, taken copious notes on all copulations.

They'd giggled a lot the first night. Joanna made jokes about buying novelization rights to one of the films, *The Plumber's Helper*, six overexposed minutes of a lonely housewife discovering the unrecognized advantages of a clogged sink. Joanna called it "deeply probing." They all agreed they'd never be able to look at a Roto-Rooter man the same way again.

After *Horsing Around*, a gamey comedy about a group of exuberant equestrians learning to ride a cowboy, Karen said that she was going home to rape her vibrator. Even Sonni, who took the whole matter much more seriously, found herself turned on and laughing unnecessarily loudly at the in-the-dugout antics of two energetic blondes in *Double Play*. But that was the first night.

By the fifth night the films had all the erotic power of parthenogenesis.

Joanna and Karen groaned each time Sonni reloaded the projector, but she ignored them. If they aimed to be successful, they had to know their field.

"Baseball players have to sit through endless reruns of plays if they want to improve their game," Sonni said as *Hot Toddy* began to roll. "Even brain surgeons have to watch training films."

Sounding a little like Boris Karloff, Karen said, "A good old-fashioned lobotomy would be a relief."

Joanna agreed. She had taken to giving fashion commentaries on the actors' clothes before they took them off.

Sonni reminded them that they weren't going into business for laughs. "We're selling something," she said. "And if we want customers, we have to know exactly *what* we're selling and precisely *how* to sell it. Cost efficiency is a prime consideration."

Karen pointed to the screen. A waitress was going down on a short-order cook as he made flapjacks. "What's that have to do with cost efficiency?" she asked.

"Everything. If we're offering moderately priced sex, we have to know the most effective way to do it in the least amount of time. We're not catering to special tastes. We're dealing with the average man."

"I've gone to bed with a lot of average men," Joanna said, "but there are still different strokes for different folks."

The short-order cook hoisted the waitress's skirt and bent her over the sink.

"But not all *that* different," Sonni persisted. "Foreplay is where variation comes in, but we're not emphasizing that. We're providing no-frills sex."

The short-order cook was now pumping away. The waitress's breasts dipped jiggling into a sinkful of soap bubbles. Karen excused herself and went to the refrigerator for a diet soda.

"There has to be *some* foreplay," Joanna protested. Never having experienced orgasm, she held foreplay in very high regard. "It can't just be lights off, and hard on."

"Of course not," Sonni agreed. "We'll provide foreplay, but it has to be fast-acting and effective."

"Sounds like Alka-Seltzer," said Karen, returning with her soda and a jar of peanut butter.

The waitress turned and put her legs around the cook's waist; his hands were on her buttocks. As he pulled her in, the camera cut to another waitress, who eyed the scene, stroking a carrot.

"Look," Sonni explained, "we're going to reduce all this stuff"—she indicated the screen—"to a reliable, basic five-minute preamble that'll work with any main course."

"Where'd you come up with five minutes?" Joanna wanted to know.

"By subtraction." Sonni looked at her yellow pad. "I did some calculations last night. I figure a total of twenty minutes in the bedroom. Allowing three and a half for undressing, four and a half for dressing, and seven for the act itself, that leaves five for foreplay. End of sex. Then five minutes to make the omelette, ten to eat it, and we can have them in bed, out of bed, and well fed in thirty-five minutes. We have to think in terms of quick turnover."

The waitress with the carrot allied herself with the cook, who was now servicing the cashier too. They all took turns flipping pancakes on the griddle.

"Thirty-five minutes." Joanna whistled. "That's expecting fast action from strangers, isn't it?"

"They won't be paying for small talk. Customers aren't interested in your favorite restaurant or what you thought about Woody Allen's last movie. Really, if guys didn't feel obligated to comment on the books in our apartments or say all those other things they do when they get there, just so we won't think they're there for the one reason they *are*, they'd probably come and go in less time than it takes us to get them there in the first place."

"That's no-frills all right," Joanna admitted.

"There are lots of ways we can save time when you stop to think about it," Sonni said.

"They could always start without us," Karen suggested.

"I'm serious," Sonni said. "Instead of using up the clock trying to figure out what guys want, we'll have a menu. They can order by number."

"By number? Isn't that a little impersonal?"

"We're selling sex, not life insurance."

Karen shook her head. "I don't know. I'm better at names than numbers."

"Then we'll have both," Sonni said. By the end of the evening, they did.

The menu offered five selections, available in blonde, brunette, or redhead (Sonni would buy the wigs), and featured five omelettes.

It looked like this:

WHAT'S COOKING
"Where your pleasure is our business"

SPECIALTIES OF THE HOUSE

#1   His .... $100.
(our wholesome, old-fashioned missionary
position)

#2   Hers .... $100.
(a delightful variation for the easy
going, with the woman on top)

#3   Poochie .... $100.
(a favorite of all nature's cuddly creatures
and men of hindsight everywhere)

*All above orders include What's Cooking's special
Foreplay—a delicious blending of oral and manual talents
to excite the appetite.*

EXTRA ADDED ATTRACTIONS

#4   Lollipop .... $75.
(a lipsmacking treat that can't be beat)

#5   Handyman's Delight .... $25.
(our time- and money-saving manual)

- PLEASE SPECIFY BLONDE, BRUNETTE, OR REDHEAD
- COMBINATIONS AVAILABLE FOR TWICE THE PRICE
- OMELETTES ON THE HOUSE.

Omelettes
Plain, Cheese, Mushroom, Spinach, Tomato
(We show you how to make 'em the way you like 'em.)

"We're going to need quite a staff," Joanna pointed out.

"And a lot of vitamins," added Karen, spreading peanut butter on a large piece of pita bread.

Sonni said, "I don't expect staff to be a problem. I've made a few discreet calls and I think we'll have enough bedroom help to keep the place open through rain, snow, sleet, transit strikes, and Jewish holidays. Everyone I spoke to was wild about the idea."

"Really?" Joanna was amazed.

"Well . . . maybe not *everyone.*" Four callees had hung up on her, and her old friend Royce Barnett, a lab technician at Pfizer who took pills to augment virtually all her bodily functions and had screwed and been screwed by more researchers than it took to develop ampicillin, had called her a tramp.

On the other hand, Andrea Nackman had called her a genius.

Chapter 8

"I think it's a breakthrough in sexual economics," Andrea said the following week, when they met for lunch. "Dazzlingly liberal. I'm impressed."

"Honestly?" Sonni brightened. Andrea was not easily impressed by the ideas of others. In many ways she was a lot like her husband Bernard, who had recently been unimpressed by a Hollywood executive's suggestion that Bernard's talent should be the subject of his next disaster movie.

"My God, yes," Andrea said. "When I think of the year I tried to make some money that Bernardo wouldn't know about by selling Mary Kay cosmetics, I could positively shoot myself." She cut a piece of quiche and held it on her fork. "It's going to be a lot easier to sell one man a hundred-dollar lay than ten women a five-dollar jar of moisturizer."

"The house takes twenty percent."

"That's still better than pushing night creams, believe me."

"I hope so," said Sonni. The past few evenings she'd been nettled with doubts about the school, even though she'd come to thinking of it as Destiny's Design. She'd tried to tell herself that they were nothing more than anticipatory jitters, but could not shake the gnawing feeling that she might be pursuing the same sort of pipe dream that had propelled her father headlong into No-Hands Floor Mops and then clobbered him.

Irv Mishkin has been so sure he could clean up on No-Hands mops, which were strapped to the feet and then skated over the floor, that he'd taken out loans amounting to well over twenty-five thousand dollars to manufacture and distribute his "answer to a housewife's prayer" himself. The first housewife to break her pelvis brought the Better Business Bureau down on him; the second brought a lawsuit that forced him to sell their house and become a Good Humor Ice Cream Man for two years.

"I'm telling you," Andrea said in her practiced debutante whisper, "men are going to love it."

"I know they're going to love it, but will they pay a hundred bucks for it? Freebies are a dime a dozen. I can't play Lysistrata at all the singles bars."

"Pet, where have you been? It costs more than a hundred for a decent date these days. Dinner, drinks—and then in the end it's still a gamble. You're offering men a sure thing." Andrea lit a cigarette and puffed contemplatively. "I see it all as very . . . humanitarian. My coming into the city on Tuesdays and Wednesdays will be like doing charity work—with remuneration." Andrea's

Junior League training never failed her; she could elevate vivisection to mercy killing and gang bangs to communal sex.

"I'd volunteer for Thursdays too," she said, "but that's when Bernard plays tennis and it's my only night to be . . . well, legitimately free." She smiled serenely. "I don't want to screw up my love life."

"How is Henry-John, by the way?"

"Still in traction."

"Traction?"

"Oh, I didn't tell you." She made a face. "My thousand-dollar toy is decorating a pine tree off the Ellenville cliffs. Henry-John caught a crosswind on his first jump."

"Will he be all right?"

Andrea shrugged. "I suppose so. Bastards heal fast."

"Bastard? From free-spirited primal poet to bastard? That was a quick one. What happened?"

"He blamed the accident on the glider, called it crummy, which is to say he blamed me. The one thing I can't take is guilt. It devastates me."

Andrea did not look devastated, but Sonni was concerned. "Listen, are you sure you can handle working at the school?"

"What's that have to do with guilt?"

"Well . . . you *are* married, and . . ."

"It's not like I'll be doing it for *fun*, for God's sake. It'll be a real hassle freeing those Tuesday and Wednesday nights."

"Okay. Just thought I'd better check. Can you come into town next Monday for the training session?"

"Training session?" Andrea laughed, tapped her cigarette against the ashtray. "I don't know whether to take that as a compliment or an insult."

"It's for all personnel, regardless of experience," Sonni

said. "Consistency is important. Everyone has to be able to do the same things the same way." She described the five-minute foreplay.

Andrea snuffed out her cigarette, holding it for a long moment. "Hmmm," she said.

"What's wrong?"

"Oh, nothing."

Of course something was, and Sonni nailed it immediately: the school's necessary standardization. It was anathema to women like Andrea, who prided themselves on the uniqueness of their sexual prowess; who believed that all their social, academic, and domestic inadequacies were compensated for by their incomparable performances in bed. Andrea, who wrote poor poetry, told lame jokes, and didn't know one end of a vacuum cleaner from another, considered herself a diva of oral sex. She'd be a definite asset to the school, but only if she could be convinced that uniformity of product was essential for success.

"Look," Sonni explained, "with the price of butter, eggs, and gynecologists, our overhead just doesn't allow for superstars. Bluntly: we've got to get customers in, off, and out in less than an hour."

"What you're saying, then, is that it's essentially a fast-fuck operation."

"I suppose you could call it that if you want to," Sonni said defensively.

"I don't want to," Andrea said, "but you have to admit it doesn't smack of romance."

"If they want romance, they can screw Barbara Cartland."

Sonni returned late to the office. A dozen well-dressed men in wheelchairs were in the reception area. They had come from as far south as Georgia and as far west as Montana for a shot at WCBN's weatherperson slot. Most of them were smoking or talking quietly. Two were playing bluff poker with dollar bills. One was oiling his wheels with W-D 40. They all appeared to be veterans of countless waiting rooms. None looked as if he could tell a satellite photo from a street map of Poughkeepsie. As it turned out, only one of them could: George Wilkins.

Sonni marched into Albie Drury's office to tell him that they had a problem. She avoided Tina, whose toeless, six-foot-two cousin had been the notable exception. While the man was practically a human barometer, could read clouds and wind velocities the way architects read blueprints, and had an idiot savant's recall of how much snow had fallen where on any given date in the last hundred years, he wasn't legitimately handicapped.

"I don't even know if Tina was telling the truth about his toes," said Sonni, keeping her voice low. "He admitted that he'd rented the chair just for the interview."

"Hmmm." Albie tapped a pencil on his nose. "How did he look in it?"

"In what?"

"In the wheelchair."

Sonni shrugged, confused. "Like he was sitting."

"I mean, could he pass?"

"Pass?"

"For a paraplegic."

"Albie!" Sonni gasped. "We can't do that."

"Why not? Upstairs wants a weatherperson in a wheelchair, so we'll give 'em a good one."

"But he can walk perfectly."

"We'll pay him not to."

"Viewers will get to know him. What if he decides to take a stroll one day and someone sees him? We could lose all our credibility. What would people think if—"

"They'll think just what we want them to think."

"Huh?"

"They'll think it's a *miracle*," said Albie, smiling and fondling his pencil. He stood, faced the window, then whirled toward Sonni. "And if we play it right, we can have it happen live on the *Nightly News*."

"So, do we have a new weatherperson?" Ernie Hemmingway asked her that night in the elevator.

"I guess," said Sonni, not wanting to get into it.

Ernie worked too closely with Van Danner, De Lucca, and Le Berman for candor. It was generally accepted that downstairs keep upstairs uninformed whenever possible. And vice versa. Sonni learned more about WCBN at lunch with friends from other networks than she ever did at the office.

When they reached the street, a voice behind Sonni said, "You look like you could use a drink. How about it?" She started to turn, then remembered how Ernie could throw his voice. She grinned at him. "I could, and I'd love to," she said.

He was startled. "I beg your pardon?"

"I—Didn't you . . ?" She looked over her shoulder and saw a woman take the arm of the man who had offered the invitation. Sonni's cheeks flushed. Embarrassed, she turned slowly back to Ernie. "I'm sorry," she began, "I thought—" She didn't have to say any more. Ernie Hemmingway had vanished again.

In the cab on the way downtown she tried to decide whether Ernie was either very rude or very shy, and couldn't. This disturbed her, because she was good at making decisions. It was an ability she was proud of, a hard-learned ability that had been carefully cultivated in her by her father. One of Irv Mishkin's favorite expressions, which he used without fail or forethought whenever Sonni was undecided about what to order in a restaurant or what dress to wear, was, "No one ever got to the top on a maybe." He had inculcated decisiveness by relentlessly drawing upon such examples as "Did Rockefeller say 'Maybe' when they asked if they could name a center after him?" or "Did Arthur Fiedler say 'Maybe' when they asked him to conduct the Boston Pops?" or "Did Michelangelo say 'Maybe' when they asked him to paint a ceiling?" When Sonni protested that sometimes a maybe was called for, that occasionally hedging was the best course of action, her father would shout, "If Thomas Edison's mother had said 'Maybe' to his father, we'd all still be sitting in the dark." Irv Mishkin's logic was as specious as it was irrefutable, and was so drummed into Sonni that she gradually accepted it as part of the same paternal legacy that had given her the upturned Mishkin nose. She had made many mistakes in her life, but she'd never once hesitated to make them. She decided not to make a decision about Hemmingway. No one really understood the man, anyway.

She got out at Fourteenth Street. Near Eighth Avenue the block steamed with a tired, damp throng of after-work shoppers. The makeshift stalls set out in front of stores offered bargains to anyone looking for size-ten turquoise sandals, old Guy Lombardo albums, polyester kimonos, or extra-large underwear. The heat was oppressive, as oppressive as Sonni's thoughts when she looked at the oversized underwear and thought of Flossie Gerber, the only woman who could probably smother a Living Bra to death.

The woman had Irv Mshkin so revved in sexual frenzy that Sonni couldn't even listen to her father anymore without imagining Flossie's heavy breathing in the background.

At Flossie's instigation he had sold his beautiful oak four-poster and purchased a mechanized bed designed to ripple the body at a push of the button and give an emergency-room look to ordinary apartments. He had also taken to drinking his coffee black and putting plastic covers on the lampshades, and had switched from cigars to thin red Nat Sherman cigarettes, which Flossie had convinced him added color to his face.

The woman was Machiavelli in Spandex.

Or was she? Sonni had to admit that her father was happy these days, happier than she'd ever known him to be. All he seemed to talk about was his *wonderful* Gerber Baby, all the *wonderful* things she did.

It distressed Sonni to think that she might possibly have misjudged Flossie—distressed her even more when she considered that her continuing distaste for the woman might have little to do with the way she handled Irv or even her unstoppable upsmanship; that it might spring from nothing more than having lost out on a bus seat.

She tried to push Flossie from her mind, but it was a lot to push. By the time she got to the wig store, a now-familiar headache had begun.

Mr. Hair was a narrow store, no wider than the subway cars that ran beneath it. On a banner above the rest room it boasted, "THE LARGEST SELECTION OF WIGS, FALLS AND CHIGNONS ANYWHERE." The place was run by a small Italian man named Vito, who had tacked to the wall dozens of autographed glossies of celebrities acclaiming his hairpieces. Burt Reynolds had written, "To Vito, the tops in tops, All the best, Burt;" Dolly Parton's said, "Hair's to ya, Vito, Love, Dolly;" Roy Rogers' said, "Thanks, Vito, my hat never fit so good." Sonni noted that the handwriting on all the photographs was the same as that on the sign by the cash register advising patrons that no checks were accepted.

Vito excused himself from an undecided customer and approached Sonni with a smile. "I've covered the best heads in the business," he said, indicating the photos on the wall. "Whatever you're looking for, I've got. And if I don't got, I'll get. And if I can't get, you're out of luck." He laughed, and picked a piece of food from his teeth with his thumbnail. He was slim and wore tight pale-blue slacks that looked as if they'd been designed for a eunuch. They left no doubt about the wearer's gender, but effectively squelched any chance of his arousal. "What kind of head are you into?" he asked.

"Well, I need . . . um . . . an assortment," Sonni said.

"You've come to the right place," he assured her. "I've got 'em in Dynel, Arnel, whatever you want, from hemp up to the real thing." Making a rectangle with his fingers, he looked at Sonni. "You'd make one helluva blonde," he said. Before she could respond, he took a long golden wig from a faceless head and handed it to her. "Here, try it on."

"I—"

"Go on," he urged, turning her toward the mirror.

Sonni shrugged, put on the wig, and then simply stared at herself. The change was remarkable. No longer was she the crisp assignments editor who wore tailored suits, read *The New Yorker* cover to cover, kept her nails efficiently short, took cold showers, and ate Wheaties every morning for breakfast. Suddenly she was Cinderella, Suzanne Sommers, a homecoming queen, a *Playboy* Playmate who ate ice-cream cones in hot tubs, adored big men in little sports cars, whose secret dream was to be stranded on a Greek

island with a French count. It was unbelievable what hair
could do.

"You like?" Vito asked. He winked, then turned side-
ways and coughed as he tugged at his slacks. Sonni pretended not to notice.

"I'll take it, but I'll need some others too."

"Ah." Vito nodded knowingly. "A woman of many
moods. Don't worry, we have hair for all occasions." He
led her to the rear, where there was shelf upon shelf of
disembodied heads, a Grand Guignol assortment of faceless blondes, brunettes, and redheads.

Sonni was thrilled. With the right wigs, a staff of six
could promote the appearance of a dozen. Vito gave her a
mirror and told her to take her time. He asked only that
she replace the wigs on their proper stands. He liked, he
said, to keep his heads in the right place.

Each wig Sonni tried on surprised her with a new per-
sonality. Wearing a long dark wig, she saw herself as a
sultry Latin who could make men perspire at a glance. An
elaborately banana-curled blond upsweep gave her the
appearance of a bawdy country-and-Western singer. Both
images had market potential. A short brown wig with
bangs turned out to be a disappointment. She was hoping
for a fetching, innocent young Brigitte Bardot look, but
got one more resembling Mamie Eisenhower. She put it
back. She couldn't imagine anyone paying for sex with
Mamie Eisenhower.

After two hours, she had selected nine wigs and seen
herself as enough women to single-handedly satisfy the
National League. She decided to wear the long blond wig
home just for a lark.

She paid for her purchases and was preparing to leave
when she noticed a good-looking bald man in one-way
sunglasses standing in the corner. She stopped and

pretended to search for something in her purse, sneaking another glance as she did. Ordinarily she wouldn't have given him a second look. Bald men reminded her of her father or intelligent aliens in science-fiction movies, neither of which excited her sexually. But there was something about the man that was definitely pheromonic, that sparked her libido in a curious fashion and caused her to smile at him as brazenly as a Playmate would at a French count. The man grinned and ran his tongue over his lips. It was not the response of a French count. Sonni bolted from the store.

Her face remained flushed all the way home. What had possessed her to do that? The wig? Long golden hair was no excuse for acting like a tramp, which was undoubtedly what the man thought she was. But what was there about him that had triggered such an action, and why had it felt so natural?

Inside her apartment she poured herself a Scotch and thought about it. Everything she thought distressed her.

Perhaps she'd been deluding herself for years about her real feelings for bald men. After seeing *The King and I*, she had, in retrospect, spent several sexually satisfying nights in fantasy with Yul Brynner. And once, after a particularly good *Kojak*, she did use Telly Savalas for a pleasurable rape. Was it her father that she'd really wanted on these occasions? Were Yul Brynner and Telly Savalas merely surrogates for Irv Mishkin? She probed her psyche relentlessly, digging at it with Freud, poking it with Reich, becoming it with Gestalt, but still found the connection unlikely; as unlikely as pleasurable rape.

Something about the man continued to bother her, but it was as elusive as a tiny ant crawling on her back. She decided to take a shower and forget the whole thing, which was when the truth fell into place.

Reaching for her shower cap, she bumped the shelf that held her toiletries, which sent a box of rose-scented disposable douche tumbling across the floor. She picked it up, remembering the time she'd been asked to read the label on a Trailways bus, and suddenly it was as if someone had smashed the ant on her back and driven a fist right through to her guts.

Of course! It had to be he. Though bald as a grapefruit, the man behind those one-way sunglasses had been none other then Wyatt Stelson, the People's Person, the sonofabitch she'd vowed to hate forever. It infuriated her that she hadn't recognized him immediately. Her only comfort was that at least she hadn't smiled at a total stranger.

Chapter 9

"All right, girls," Sonni shouted at the group, "that's enough with the wigs." She heard the sharpness in her voice and was annoyed with herself for being annoyed. But it was understandable. She had counted on twelve permanent employees, enough so that there never would be a chance of having fewer women than the number of bedrooms on any given night. But five of her definites had backed out in the last week, which left seven, and the opening was only two days away.

Besides that, the dry run was going badly.

"I love me as a brunette." Andrea whirled so that the hair flared out. "It makes me feel like dancing . . . dancing."

"We're not opening an Arthur Murray studio," Sonni said. "Would all of you just put those things away."

Karen, wearing short blond curls, broke from three others who were delightedly exchanging hairpieces. "My God, Sonni, these wigs are fabulous. I'll bet even the guys I know wouldn't recognize me." She primped the curls. "All I need is a pinafore and I could play Shirley Temple." She began to sing "On the Good Ship Lollipop."

"Swell. If we get any nine-year-olds, they're yours." Sonni stood in front of the fireplace and clapped her hands. "Come on, friends, we're wasting too much time on the packaging."

"What's more important?" asked Sheryl Keef with real indignation.

Sheryl, whom Sonni had known when she worked for Durkin and Durkin, was a devout advertising executive and personally responsible for the repackaging and soaring sales of several products, including an antiperspirant that had been around for years and an ineffective lemon-scented bug spray. As she'd told Sonni, who had once complained about the bug spray and couldn't understand its success, "It's what the public sees, not what it gets, that counts." A short, quick-thinking, volatile young woman with family money and an unfortunate mole on her right nostril, Sheryl had volunteered for What's Cooking because as she'd said, she was much too involved with her job to consider marriage or an affair. She viewed sex as an essential bodily function and felt that doing it two nights a week would be good for her.

"In this business there are more important things," Sonni said.

"In *this business,*" Sheryl protested, "the right packaging is vital. No guy's going to pay for something that doesn't look good."

"Let me put it this way," Sonni said patiently. "A guy might be turned on by a beautiful Porsche or Ferrari, but if he gets behind the wheel and it doesn't perform, no amount of chrome or Polyglycoat is going to get him to buy it."

"Sonni's right," declared Chris Conway. She was a tall striking blonde and former est leader. Two years ago she'd taken a job as a receptionist for a large law firm, and recently had begun making pronouncements like a judge.

"I think so, too," said Evelyn Stang, a secretary in charge of the Xerox machines at the same law firm.

"I'm inclined to side with Sheryl." Andrea was now wearing Karen's Shirley Temple curls and admiring herself.

"Christ, we didn't come here to debate," Joanna said wearily. She'd had to break a date with a lieutenant from the Sixth Precinct and was feeling out of sorts.

"That's right," said Chris.

"You can say that again," murmured Evelyn.

"Thank you," said Sonni. "Maybe now we can get somewhere." She pushed up her sleeves. "Okay. We all have the omelettes down pat." The women applauded. It was the first indication of real team spirit. "Now if you just think of the Handyman's Delight as an extended version of the wrist action you use in cracking an egg, it'll be perfect. Some of you still need to work on your number fours. I think what Karen told you about swordswallowers is a good thing to remember. And Andrea's suggestion about practicing breath control with a cucumber should be kept in mind. But I'm afraid we're going to have to run through foreplay again."

There were groans.

Sonni held up her hand. "Look, I know it's only an accouterment, but that's what's going to make our customers believe they're getting something special for their money. I mean, what's a Gucci belt without the "G" on the buckle? A piece of leather. Nobody'd pay a hundred bucks just to keep his pants up—or take them down for that price—unless they're getting something worthwhile."

Sheryl raised her hand. "I keep forgetting," she said, "whether we go from the feet up or the waist down, or is it from the waist up and then the neck down?"

"Just remember that nothing goes up if you start from the top," Sonni said, "whether it's a number one, two, or three, you get into foreplay feet first."

"Do we have to say that *bone* thing when they enter the room?" asked Evelyn Stang, crinkling her face like a piece of Xerox paper caught in the machine.

"It's *bon*, not bone. *Bon appétit!* It means enjoy your meal." Sonni had thought it a nice touch, sort of in keeping with the omelettes.

"I find that *très* cute," said Andrea, who often dabbed French like Dijon mustard on her remarks. "But I must confess that I'm not in love with having to say 'Come again' when the guy leaves the room. He might take it literally."

Evelyn asked what Andrea meant. Sheryl leaned over and explained quietly.

Sonni began to wonder if Evelyn was going to work out. High IQs weren't a prerequisite, but someone slow on the uptake could get into trouble—get them all into trouble. Though Evelyn was physically experienced, having been the Mostess Hostess at Camp Lettingo, an adult retreat in the Poconos where copulation was the only structured activity, she was basically afraid of men, convinced that an improperly handled aroused male would kill to get into a woman's pants, and a total innocent when it came to the ramifications of sex. She'd done terribly on the written exam.

Sonni had devised the exam for prospective employees because she believed, as any baseball manager did, that there was more to being a pitcher than knowing how to throw the ball. You had to be able to read signs.

The test was multiple choice and had five questions. The five questions were:

1. If a man says, "I'm into water sports," it means (a) he's a scuba diver and wants to take you to the Bahamas; (b) he wants to fool around in the bathtub; (c) he's interested in kinky diversions that we're neither equipped nor inclined to handle.

2. When a man makes a reference to "French," he's referring to (a) pastries; (b) postcards; (c) oral sex.

3. If, during an order, a customer asks, "Am I hurting you?," he expects you to say (a) "Are you kidding?" (b) "Not as much as the last guy;" (c) "Yes (bravely) . . . a little."

4. At any point during an order, if a man says, "Ohmygod, ohmygod," or "Jeezus, Jeezus," it means (a) he's having a religious experience; (b) he's just remembered that he's forgotten his wife's birthday; (c) he'll be ready for his omelette in a few minutes.

5. At any point after disrobing, if a man says, "Oh, that, it's just a heat rash," you (a) put talcum powder on him; (b) put cold water on him; (c) put your clothes back on, and split.

Evelyn had marked (a) and (b) all the way down. Sonni had her take the test again. She finally passed on her third try, which was a pretty poor showing for the Mostess Hostess from Camp Lettingo.

Sonni looked at her watch. "All right," she said. "It's getting late. We'll forgo the foreplay run-through, but I think you should all practice. Go through the motions at home.

Andrea sighed. "That's *all* I do at home."

Evelyn laughed, which heartened Sonni somewhat.

"Do we still want a cat?" Karen asked.

"Definitely. It's the perfect touch. Besides, it'll look peculiar if we don't have one. I've already put a litter box in the bathroom."

"Okay, I'll donate Mouse."

"Mouse?"

"She's my cat. She's great, doesn't shed, doesn't jump up and purr all over you, doesn't claw the furniture or run around meowing all the time. She's just sort of . . ."

"Dead?" Evelyn offered.

Karen scowled. "Laid back."

"She sounds great," Sonni said quickly. "Bring her on Friday. Which reminds me, all of you should be here around seven. Even those who've bid weekends off."

"How come?" asked Chris, who went to the Hamptons on weekends with a couple that she occasionally slept with.

"We've got to look impressive," explained Joanna. She'd already bought a new Halston dress and perfume for the first night. "After all, a grand opening is a grand opening."

"It's so *merveilleux*," said Andrea. "I can't wait to see our first customers—or are they clients?"

"Clients," said Chris, who called people that every day.

"Customers," said Karen, always keeping the box office in mind.

"Johns," said Joanna, eschewing euphemism.

"Balls!" shouted Sonni, who suddenly realized that

she'd been so involved in getting the women ready she'd forgotten all about arranging to bring in the men.

"It was just an oversight. Could have happened to anyone," Karen said after everyone but her and Joanna had left. She patted Sonni's shoulder like a trainer in a grade-B fight film. "We can still do it in time."

"Sure we can," Joanna called encouragingly from the kitchen, where she'd just completed stocking boxes of eggs in the refrigerator.

"I have the feeling that Xaviera and Polly Adler didn't start this way," Sonni said disconsolately. "How could it have slipped my mind?"

"Who has time to think about men when they're busy?"

"Cheer up," Joanna said, stopping by the mirror to fix her hair. "I'll slip a word to one of my friends at the Seventy-sixth and we'll have enough clients up here to stop a riot."

"Policemen?" Sonni shook her head.

"Why not?" Joanna said defensively. "They have the same urges as stockbrokers."

"But not the same bankroll," Karen interjected. "Show me the cop who's going to pay a hundred bucks for a cheese omelette and a piece of ass."

"Well . . ."

"They're used to perks, payoffs, freebies. And what do we do if they don't want to pay—call the cops? Christ, Joanna, they could bust us before we've even seasoned our pans."

"Unlikely," said Joanna. "I'm on intimate terms with the chief."

"That's what John Dean and Agnew said."

Joanna threw up her hands. "Okay, okay. I only offered to help. But I'll tell you, you could do a lot worse than go to bed with a cop."

"I probably have," said Karen, who probably had; her eclectic roster of bed partners included a sixty-three-year-old chimp trainer from Louisville and a seventeen-year-old exchange student from La Paz, Bolivia.

With a surprising modicum of passion that was quite becoming, Joanna said, "They're a hell of a lot better than businessmen, lawyers, or artists, who spend half their time analyzing relationships or half their money paying someone else to, believe me. Cops don't take it personally if you don't have an orgasm. They don't make you feel guilty, less of a woman. You never have to fake it. They don't really care. It's a great relief." They also, she said, didn't have the romantic compulsion of businessmen, lawyers, and artists to run their fingers through your hair, which, at forty bucks a clip at Cinandre, was something to consider. "At least with cops you don't have to choose betwen looking good and getting laid."

"Well, no one's going to have to worry about that choice on Friday if we don't have any customers," said Sonni. "Damn!" She began to pace the room, her hands clasped behind her back. She looked morose, like a coach whose team was behind six to two at the bottom of the ninth.

"I know a few guys who are really good sports. They might come just for the hell of it," Karen offered.

"Hmmm." Sonni thought a moment. "How many?"

"Two—maybe three. I don't know about Arnold. A guy who brings you a bottle of Scotch, then takes home what you don't finish at the end of the evening, doesn't strike me as the sort to pay for something he doesn't have to."

"What about the others?"

Karen waved her hand. "Paul and Dennis? Oh, they're spenders. Paul is Panglow Films. I've seen him brush his teeth with a gram of coke just for laughs. And Dennis is a very successful plastic surgeon. Actually, I'm sure I can get Dennis. He's an obsessive consumer—two boats, two BMWs, three or four condominiums. He likes buying things, it makes him feel secure. He doesn't appreciate anything that doesn't cost him something. His first wife didn't ask for a cent when they split, and he thinks she's a schmuck. His second wife leeched him for a bundle, and he's still saying that she was the best thing that ever happened to him."

"Okay," Sonni said. "Get hold of them. Ask them each to tell two friends, and have the friends ask two friends. It might work if we can get it snowballing."

"It'll work even if we just get Paul and Dennis. They're big spenders."

"That's fine, but there's a limit to how many omelettes a guy can eat."

Chapter 10

Sonni felt as if she'd swallowed a flock of butterflies. She hadn't been so nervous since her wedding night, when she knew that bed and the moment of truth were approaching and that she wasn't ready for the reckoning.

Lenny Rubin had endured a year of settling for first, second, and third base because he believed Sonni was a virgin. He also believed that marrying someone who wasn't a virgin was like paying retail for damaged goods, even if he himself had done the damage. Sonni felt that she hadn't exactly lied to Lenny; she'd never said she was a virgin. Of course, she'd never said she wasn't, either.

She confessed this tearfully to her father the morning of the wedding.

"I'm marrying him under false pretenses," she wailed.

"You're marrying him under a *chuppa*," Irv Mishkin said. "And once you say 'I do, I do' to each other, it's done. When a man buys a house, does the seller point out every leak in the basement?"

"*Daddy!*" Sonni began crying again.

Irv Mishkin put an arm around her, brushed her chin with his knuckles. "Hey, Son, come on. What's to cry? When you go to a department store and see a dress you like, you buy it, right?"

Sonni nodded.

"Do you ask the salesgirl how many other people have tried it on? If it looks good, who cares?"

"We're talking about sex, not Saks. Lenny cares. I know he does. What am I going to do?"

"What are you going to do? You'll do what your mother—may she rest in peace—did."

Sonni stared at her father, shocked. "Mother wasn't a virgin?"

Irv Mishkin shrugged. "Who knew? Was I a gynecologist? She turned out the lights, gave a *kvetch*, and that was it."

"I don't want to start my marriage with a lie."

"So you're willing to end it with the truth?"

"Daddy, you don't understand. Lenny's not as understanding as you."

"Who is? Look," he said, "the whole thing is just like baseball. Does anybody get upset when the batter fools the pitcher with a bunt? It's all part of the game."

"I don't know what you're telling me."

"Bunt," he said.

That night, nervous as she was, Sonni *kvetched*, bunted, and brought in two home runs.

Now, standing in Ta'Shi's kitchen beneath Boo-Boo Palmetto's baseball bats, abstractedly greasing an omelette pan, waiting for the first customer, she wished she could speak to her father.

She'd tried to, a week before, but Flossie Gerber's oppressive presence made it impossible. The woman had taken over Irv's Dinky and was making all the arrangements for its distribution. So far nothing had happened, except that the three thousand Sonni had given to her father had disappeared; but Flossie had assured them both that it was merely a matter of time. All Sonni had been able to tell her father was that she was opening a cooking school for men, which hadn't thrilled him.

"Just omelettes? I expected more from you, Son," he'd said.

"It has . . . potential," she hedged.

He shook his head. "The American Heart Association recommends only two eggs a week. You'd be better off with hamburgers."

Flossie had interrupted at that point to say that burgers had as much dangerous cholesterol as eggs; that her son, Seymour, the vegetarian, had made the Los Angeles *Times* by staging a demonstration with stroke victims in front of Bob's Big Boy on La Cienega. Sonni dropped the subject.

She put down the omelette pan and walked into the living room to join the others. They were strangely subdued and sipping champagne. Smartly dressed in decorous street clothes (Sonni felt gowns might be intimidating), they resembled more a Haddassah group or a book club than anything else. But the tension was palpable.

"If this is the grand opening," Sheryl said, taking a long drag on a cigarette, "I can't wait to see our slow days."

"It's *only* seven-fifteen," Sonni said. "They'll be here."

Evelyn stiffened. "You know, I read in the *Enquirer*

that some guys become maniacs when they get too sexually excited . . . like they'd do anything to get into a woman's pants."

"Relax. We had ten calls, and not one of them was from Jack the Ripper."

"Eleven," Karen said, handing Sonni the appointment book.

"Great. Remember, no one gets in who hasn't called, so check names."

"That won't be difficult. They're all Smiths and Joneses—except for one Hooper."

Sonni sighed. Aliases were to be expected. Men lied for sex more routinely than politicians did for office. She looked around. "Where's Joanna?"

"She was held up at the office," Karen said. "Some big book auction. She should be here any minute."

The intercom buzzer sounded. They all fell instantly silent.

"That's probably her," Karen said easily. "I told you she'd be—"

"Joanna has a key," Sonni said slowly, "and the doorman knows her."

Karen nodded. "That's true."

"It—it must be one of *them*," Evelyn said.

"I certainly hope so," muttered Andrea, who tended toward pique when kept waiting. Stores in which she had to take a number made her outright surly.

Another buzz.

Sonni straightened her shoulders and marched toward the intercom. She pressed the talk button. "Yes?"

The doorman announced that a Mr. Jonathan Smith was there for a cooking lesson.

"Jonathan Smith?" Sonni glanced at Karen, who was looking at the book.

"There are a lot of Smiths," Karen said, nervously running her finger up and down the page.

"Well, one's as good as another as far as I'm concerned," said Andrea. "Get him up here already."

Sonni told the doorman okay. She faced the room. "All right, girls, this is it. Remember, team spirit counts, and—"

The door opened and Joanna entered. "I'm sorry I'm late," she said, going to the mirror and taking out her compact. "We were in for a million five on the Khrushchev sex scandal book and I couldn't leave till they closed—damn, I can't find my mascara."

"One's coming up right now," Sonni said quietly.

"One what?"

"Customer."

"Client," Sheryl corrected, joining Joanna at the mirror.

"Already?" Joanna looked stricken.

"It's about time," said Andrea. She was refilling her glass when the doorbell rang. She jumped, and spilled champagne on the couch. She cursed loudly.

"Shhh," Sonni said. She didn't want their first customer to get the wrong idea about the kind of women they were. Standing by the door, she looked back at the room. Her cadre stared at her as if waiting for a command. "Animate. Animate," she whispered, urging them with her hands.

Karen tossed her head and gave a small affected laugh. Chris Conway began discussing Ta'Shi's wall hangings with no one in particular. Andrea turned up the stereo and started humming along with Paul McCartney. Sheryl and Joanna pretended to chat about Vitamin C. Evelyn Stang, her eyes wide and looking as if she were about to be run through by a Watusi spear, sat frozen on the couch.

"Come on," Sonni mouthed desperately. "Move . . . talk."

Evelyn blinked twice and stood. She fluffed her red wig, licked her lips, and began to laugh gaily, as if she'd just heard a very witty joke. Then she fainted.

"Shit!" Sonni cried.

The doorbell rang again.

Evelyn was crumpled between the coffee table and the couch. Karen and Chris rushed over and tried to lift her.

"Uh-um . . . just a minute," Sonni called to the door, then hurried to help with Evelyn.

"What are we going to do?" Chris whispered.

"Get her out of here. Fast."

"Maybe I should slap her face," said Karen, whose knowledge of first aid came from late-night movies. She began to swat her fingers against Evelyn's cheeks.

"You're hurting her," Chris said.

"I am not."

"You're leaving marks."

"She doesn't feel it." As if to prove it, Karen slapped her palm hard against Evelyn. She moaned.

"See," said Chris. "You're hurting her."

"I'm bringing her to."

"Take her into a bedroom," Sonni said. "We've got a man out there."

"Maybe he's a doctor?" Chris said.

"Just get her into the bedroom," Sonni growled, moving the coffee table so they could get a better grip on Evelyn.

"I'll get some cold water," Andrea offered as Evelyn was carried out.

"Be careful," Joanna said, "She's wearing silk. It might stain."

There was another ring of the doorbell.

"Oh, fine," Sonni mumbled. "Coming!" she snapped. She plumped up the pillows on the couch and moved to straighten the coffee table. Christ, the last thing she needed now was a horny male.

Joanna patted her arm. "I'll answer. Fix yourself up, you look a little—used."

Sonni tucked in her blouse as Joanna opened the door.

The man who entered was tall and slim, with thinning dark hair. He was in his early fifties and wore thick tinted glasses with tortoiseshell frames. His shirt was opened to midchest and his slacks were belted high. A leather sports jacket was slung over his shoulder. He looked like a dentist or a chiropractor. He had a wedding band on his left hand.

"I'm here for a cooking lesson?" He glanced uneasily around the room.

"You've come to the right place," Joanna assured him, leading him in.

Sonni extended her hand. "What's cooking? We're here to serve you," she said, giving the salutation she had decided to use for the business, realizing only after she'd said it that she sounded disquietingly like her father. She didn't want to think about it. "Can I get you a glass of champagne?"

"Sure, I guess . . . I mean, why the hell not?" He smiled nervously as he took the glass. "Is this—um— extra?"

"Extra? Oh, no, it's on the house." She smiled. "I'm Sonni, and this is Joanna." She'd thought about using phony names, but felt it inappropriate to the school's premise of honest sex.

He nodded politely, then looked around the room. "Are you—" he pointed to both of them—"uh, are you *it?*"

"It?" Joanna looked confused.

"Part of it," Sonni said quickly, wondering what was keeping the others. Damn that Evelyn.

Mr. Smith shifted his weight, scratched his head. "Wow, *pshew,* you don't look like—like *cooks,* if you know what I mean."

Sonni assured him that she did. "Why don't you sit down," she suggested.

He shook his head. "Nah. Thanks. I sit all day. It's good for me to stand. I—I guess if I stood all day it would probably be good for me to sit." He drained his glass, and Sonni poured him another.

"Thanks." He walked uneasily around the room, picking up small objects and examining them. He studied Boo-Boo Palmetto's mounted card collection. He seemed relieved when he spotted the cat, and bent down to pet it. The cat didn't move.

"Nice cat," he said. "What's her name?"

"Mouse."

Smith laughed. "Good kitty." He scratched her stomach. Mouse's head lolled to the side. Her eyes blinked open, then closed again.

"Very affectionate," he said. "They're a lot of fun to have around—cats, I mean."

"Would you like to see where we give the lessons?" Sonni asked. "Or would you rather wait?"

"Wait? Why wait?" He put down his sports jacket and rolled up his sleeves.

Sonni led him into the kitchen. It was obviously not where Mr. Smith thought they were going. "This is it," she said.

"In here?" He looked thoroughly bewildered.

"It's cozy, don't you think?" Sonni asked. The copper pans, which hung between the baseball bats, had been shined beautifully, though she realized, when Mr. Smith bumped his head on one, that they'd have to be raised a bit higher in the future. She made a quick mental note.

"Very nice," he said. "I—um—like the baseball bats. Really nice." He nodded approvingly. "You play?"

Sonni shook her head. "I used to, when I was a kid. I never had time to practice." She looked at her watch. The ten-minute greeting period was almost over. Smith should have paid, ordered, and decided what omelette he wanted already. Karen was supposed to handle all that. Damn! She couldn't run a business this way.

"Look," she said, "the girl with the menu will be right out. But you can tell me the omelette of your choice now. We have cheese, mushroom, spinach, and plain." She took out a small pad from the drawer. "We'll have all the ingredients ready."

"Huh?" Mr. Smith looked at her as if she'd just started speaking in tongues.

"*There* you are," Karen said from the doorway.

Smith swung around, smacking his forehead on a bat, sending the bat crashing to the floor.

"Are you all right?" Sonni asked.

Smith rubbed his head where a small rosy mark was spreading. "I—I guess so." He looked at Karen and smiled.

She waited a beat; her Audrey Hepburn hesitation; then returned the smile. Moving forward, she took his hand, gave him a menu, and led him back into the living room. Sonni had to admit the girl's timing was good.

Karen returned a few minutes later with a hundred-dollar bill and a big grin. "He ordered a number two with Andrea in blond and wants a spinach omelette." She handed the bill to Sonni.

Sonni held it up against the wall. "Maybe we should frame it."

"We haven't even paid for the champagne yet," Karen said, evidencing more business sense than Sonni would have credited her with. "And so far Smith is our only customer."

"It's early." The intercom buzzer sounded in the other room. "See, what did I tell you?"

The buzzer turned out to be Lovell Florists with a potted geranium for Sonni. The plant was from her father. The message on the card covered both sides. It said:

> Hey, Son, here's to good cooking. Keep your pots clean and remember that the customer always thinks he's right but you know better. Take cash, not compliments. A penny saved is bubkas, but spent it can still get you a Chiclet. Never do tomorrow what you already did today unless it makes money. Try harder, aim higher, shoot straighter and stand taller than your competitors. Innovate when possible, imitate when profitable, and don't take any wooden nickles.
>
> Your loving
> DAD

Irv Mishkin had never been a man of few words. Sonni wondered if the message would have been longer or shorter if he knew the real nature of her business.

She put the plant on the piano and joined Joanna, who was organizing utensils for Mr. Smith's omelette lesson. If Andrea was working on schedule, Smith would be ejaculating and ready to cook in about six minutes.

It turned out that he was four minutes late, but, as

Andrea said to Sonni after Smith had gone, "You have to allow a little leeway when they're over fifty."

Sonni decided to allow them thirty seconds a year.

She also decided to give the girls a pep talk before the next customer arrived. Her team just wasn't giving their all to the game.

"Men need to be titillated," she told them. "But they also need to feel secure and unthreatened to perform." She drew an unthinking analogy to the mating of race-horses, which offended everyone except Evelyn, who remained unconscious in one of the bedrooms, and Chris Conway, whose parents owned a two-year-old thoroughbred named Big Bucks.

"We've got to look seductive without appearing pushy."

"There's a limit to how long you can look seductive with no men around." Sheryl glanced at her watch, casting an accusing eye at Sonni.

Chris yawned. "I've had livelier times at family-circle meetings." She poured herself more champagne.

Joanna sighed. "Maybe we overestimated the male libido?"

"Look, if Smith made it, so will the others. Even the Wright Brothers didn't get off the ground on the first try." Sonni clapped her hands and turned the music louder. "Come on, let's keep our spirits up."

Chris shrugged. "We've nothing better to."

An hour later, when no further men had appeared, Chris announced that she was going home. She patted Sonni's shoulder. "It sounded like a great idea, but then so did the Edsel."

"One slow night doesn't mean we're out of the ball game," said Sonni.

"Of course not," said Chris, using her positive est trainer's tone sardonically. "Smith could always come back for seconds."

"Are you kidding?" said Andrea. "It would be easier to raise the *Titanic*."

"Enough of this," Sonni said. "Are you all quitters? The school is going to make it, and it's going to make it big."

"Be realistic," Chris said. "We've had only one customer all night."

"That's right," said Sonni, "but just remember that McDonald's started with a single hamburger."

And then the intercom began to buzz.

Chapter 11

"Whew!" said Karen during a welcome lull, "I sure hope we're not aiming for the over-one-billion mark. I'm pooped."

Men had been arriving nearly every fifteen minutes for the past two hours.

"We're understaffed," said Sonni, biting her lip. "I was afraid this might happen. Where the hell is Evelyn?"

"Still out, I guess."

There was laughter from the living room and the sizzle of butter and eggs from the kitchen. "For God's sake, get her up. She can help with the omelettes if nothing else. Besides, we need another room. Andrea has two Lollipops on hold."

The doorbell rang. "Elwyn Hooper," Sonni said, making

a check in the guest book. "I'll get the door. You can bring out the menu."

Presentation was important. She half lowered her lids and smiled as she opened the door.

"Hi! What's cook—" Speechless, she stared at Elwyn Hooper. He was short, with dark curly gray-flecked hair, and could have been a twin of WCBN's comptroller, Ernie Hemmingway. But Hemmingway didn't have a twin.

"Ernie," she gasped.

"Hello," he said.

"What are you doing here?"

"I could ask you the same question," he said easily, "but I think we both already know the answers." He looked around, studied the room as if sizing up an enemy bunker that had to be taken.

Karen rushed up, and before Sonni could even think of stopping her—or could stop to think of what else to do—had shoved a menu into Ernie's hand. "Hi, what's cooking? I'm Karen." She said it so quickly that it sounded like one word, like a Turkish drinking toast.

"Excuse me?" said Ernie.

"That's quite all right," said Karen, barreling on, the champagne and the frenzied pace of the evening causing minor lacunae in her conversation. "Would you like cheese, spinach, tomato, or plain? We're out of mushrooms."

"Huh?" said Ernie.

"How could we be out of mushrooms?" interrupted Sonni, diverted from one immediate problem by another.

"The guys have been nibbling on them while waiting to cook their omelettes." She turned to Ernie. "Did you say cheese?"

"No. Should I have?"

"Probably. It works best for beginners. Melts right in. We've had a lot of leakouts with the spinach."

Ernie looked confused. "I'm afraid I—"

Karen made a mark in the book. "Don't be afraid, cheese omelettes are a snap. I'll take your money now. A hundred even."

Ernie took a billfold from his pocket, peeled off five twenties. Karen snatched them coyly, told him to enjoy himself, winked at Sonni, and disappeared.

Sonni felt stranded, as if she were naked and trapped on an island in the center of Park Avenue.

Ernie studied the menu, and then Sonni. "Interesting."

"Look, it—it's not what you think," she said quickly.

"It's not?"

"Well, it is, but—" For a moment she felt as if she might cry. It had never occurred to her that launching What's Cooking might sink her at WCBN. She'd been fired from only one job in her life, when she was sixteen and working at the Doughnut Mix; she'd been let go for making the holes too small. Her father was disappointed and it had upset her enormously. It caused her face to break out and threw her menstrual cycle into a tailspin for months. Wonderful. That's all she needed on opening night—acne and dysmenorrhea.

She took a deep breath. "All right, so what happens now?"

"I was just about to ask you that. This is the first time I've been here."

"It's the first time anyone's been here. We just opened tonight."

"Congratulations."

"Thank you."

Karen reappeared. "We're running low on spinach too," she whispered to Sonni.

"Keep pushing the cheese. We'll reevaluate the grocery budget tomorrow."

"Check." Karen gave a small salute and headed for the kitchen.

Sonni turned back to Ernie. His face was unreadable. She forced a laugh. "I—I certainly never expected to see you here."

"That puts us on equal footing."

"Not exactly," said Sonni. "You're still management."

"So, I gather from that little exchange, are you. Let's leave it at that." He pointed to the menu. "A number one with you sounds fine."

"In blonde, brunette, or redhead?" she asked.

He reached forward and brushed a curl from her forehead. "As is," he said.

When they entered the bedroom it was dark, for which Sonni was grateful. It was one thing to know she was about to make love to Ernie Hemmingway, another thing to witness it.

What disturbed her was not that Ernie was unattractive, for he wasn't, but that he was familiar; familiar in the totally nonsexual way that doormen or elevator starters or grocers were. Men to whom she'd say "Good morning," "Good night," and "Thank you," with whom she'd occasionally banter, but who were the last in the world she'd dream of having sex with.

She closed the door quickly behind her, plunging the room into complete blackness. "*Bon appétit!*" she said.

"Lights?" asked Ernie.

"Lights?" she repeated weakly.

"Unless you plan to glow in the dark."

She laughed with difficulty. "I just thought it might be more . . . exciting this way."

"For owls, perhaps."

Reluctantly she flipped the switch, and a small candelabra went on above Boo-Boo Palmetto's photo. "There," she said, "is that—"

There was a shriek from the bed.

"Wha—" Ernie started. "*Down!*" he shouted, and hurled Sonni to the floor.

Evelyn leaped from the bed. A wet washcloth, pushed back from her forehead, covered her hair like a yarmulka. She was brandishing a brass Buddha.

"Not *my* pants, maniac!" she shrieked, and swooped down on Ernie like an enraged condor.

Before Sonni could think, move, or stop either of them, Ernie had karate-kicked the Buddha across the room and decked Evelyn with an impressive chop by his stiffened right hand. The Mostess Hostess from Camp Lettingo was out like a light.

"Ohmygod," Sonni murmured. "What have you done?"

"At the risk of immodesty, I'd say . . . saved our lives." Helping a shaky Sonni to her feet, he added, "I've seen berserkers like that in Nam."

"She's a secretary from Queens," said Sonni, stunned.

"You know her, huh?"

"She works here."

He shook his head. "You'd better check your employees a little more carefully in the future."

Sonni began rubbing Evelyn's wrist. "She . . . she was sleeping off a headache. I forgot she was in here."

Ernie shook his head again. "Booze and drugs, that's what I thought. They can turn anyone into a potential killer. I saw an eighty-year-old Vietnamese grandmother put five guys into the hospital after one Sloe Gin Fizz and two pipefuls of Hanoi hash." He bent down and pushed up Evelyn's eyelid with his thumb. "She'll be all right."

Evelyn moaned, turned her head slightly. Ernie moved cautiously to the side, his eyes never leaving the woman on the floor. "Sometimes, depending on what they've drunk or smoked, they'll come to wilder than before. You'd better move back a little. Just in case I have to put her out again."

"No!" Sonni grabbed Ernie's hand. "I'm sure she'll be fine."

Ernie shook his head. "I don't know. I don't like to take chances. Risks, yes. Chances, no."

"I'll get one of the girls to keep an eye on her." Sonni was growing increasingly uneasy. She recalled articles about men whose training in Vietnam was allegedly responsible for everything from impotence to homicide. "It'll be best."

"Okay. But I'd better wait here." He placed his foot on Evelyn's stomach.

"Ernie! What are you doing?"

"She could have a concealed weapon."

"That's ridiculous."

"That's what a buddy of mine said before he got cut by a hooker from Hanoi. The foot stays or I strip and search her right now."

Ohmygod. Evelyn would be a basket case. "Okay, okay. I'll be right back." Sonni rushed out and returned with Andrea, who'd been busier than any of the others all evening.

"Keep an eye on her," Ernie said.

"With pleasure," said Andrea, dropping into a chair.

"Are you all right?" Sonni asked.

"I never felt better," Andrea replied. "But even race car drivers take time out for pit stops."

Sonni hurried Ernie into another room. They were way behind schedule. Even if she cut two minutes of foreplay, Ernie would have to be as fast off his feet as he was on them to be in time for his omelette lesson. It was unlikely, and this distressed her. When a man paid a hundred bucks for something, he deserved all of it. Well, as her father would say, the best she could do was give it the old Mishkin try.

She kicked off her shoes as she unbuttoned her blouse. Trying to unhook her bra and wiggle out of her skirt at the same time proved difficult. Ernie, who was shirtless but still in his trousers, came over and pinned her arms to her side.

"Whoa! This isn't a relay race."

"I—I don't know what you mean," she lied. She wondered if she should start licking his ear.

"I don't like to rush my . . . meals."

"Who's rushing?" she said and unbuckled his belt. She reached for his zipper.

He grabbed her hand and pressed his thumb against her wrist, sending numbing, but not altogether unpleasant, sensations up her arm. It felt as if her arm were being hypnotized. It was, he told her later, a little trick he'd picked up in Nam, where, she supposed, it was important to know how to hypnotize people's arms.

"Now, what's this all about?" he demanded.

"Well, we're running overtime."

"Overtime? We didn't even start yet."

"I know, but we should have. It's going to louse things up in the kitchen." She glanced at her watch. "If you let go of my wrist we can start right now and you'll still make your omelette."

"I didn't come here to make an omelette."

"But you get it free with sex."

"You get a lot of things free with sex, and I didn't come here for them either." He released her and lit a cigarette.

"Damn," Sonni said. "I never figured on allowing for smoking."

"Huh?"

She explained how the orders had been timed. "The whole idea is to provide guilt-free, honest, moderately priced sex—and a hot meal—at a profit."

Ernie was visibly impressed. "Tell me more."

She did. She told him everything, from how she synthesized the multitudinous erotic gyrations of over fifty porno stars into a five-minute sex prelude as rigidly choreographed as the goose step to how she designed the menus and selected the girls.

She told him everything but how a nice girl like her happened to get into a business like this.

Ernie was a good listener. It was another byproduct of Green Beret training. He considered ears nature's early-warning system and paid attention to whatever they picked up. Though Sonni had spoken rapidly, he'd caught two grammatical errors.

"Intercourse 'with,' not 'by,' " he said gently.

Sonni slapped her forehead. "You're right, of course. I don't know what I was thinking."

"I know what I'm thinking. I'm thinking you're sitting on a gold mine," he said, the Green Beret submerging, the comptroller emerging. "If what you've just described to me really works, you're going to have more customers than you can handle."

"Of course it works. We've been running pretty much on schedule all night."

He told her that five minutes of foreplay didn't sound like enough to get a man warmed up.

"If it's enough to get an old Fiat going from a cold start, it ought to be enough for any guy."

"Men are more complex than automobiles," he said wryly.

She narrowed her eyes. "Really?"

"Really."

"Are you in the mood for sex?"

"Now? No."

"The perfect cold start." She checked her watch and smiled. "*Bon appétit!*" she said, and slowly dropped her skirt.

She had him in gear and going like sixty in four minutes flat.

"I wouldn't have believed it," he said afterward.

"Quite honestly, neither would I." Sonni had never had as extraordinary a sexual experience. There was nothing like it on the menu. She felt as if every bone in her body had melted, as if her spinal column had become a Slinky. Ernie was a veritable sexual commando, storming her every fortress with maneuvers too intricate to remember, too incredibly erotic to forget. At one point he'd thrown his voice so that it seemed as if he were above, below, and on both sides of her at the same time; at another he pressed a nerve behind her knee and sent her soaring to orgasm. When she asked him sometime later where he had learned this, he said, "In Nam."

There was a lot about that war that the public still hadn't been told.

After making his omelette—as dazzling a culinary masterpiece as Sonni had ever seen—Ernie said to her, "Your girls are using too much butter. That not only cuts into profits but ruins good eggs." He admitted that he was a gourmet cook.

He also admitted that he'd been to a lot of brothels and had never felt more comfortable paying for sex.

Sonni beamed. Ernie Hemmingway wasn't known for compliments.

"Thanks," she said. "I feel as if I've been checked over by a professional. I'll have the girls hold back on the butter."

Ernie stroked his chin. "You know," he said, "you have a good staff, but you need a bouncer."

"A bouncer?" For a moment Sonni thought he was denigrating the girls' energies, which had flagged over the evening but were still pretty impressive, all things considered.

"A bouncer; you know, someone who can handle a rough situation, should it arise."

"Oh. I never thought of that."

"And an accountant who can get you functioning at a high profit level."

"I suppose," Sonni said, "but I can't afford two more employees."

"Who said anything about two?"

"You did."

"Did I?"

"You mean . . . *you*?" Sonni's eyes widened.

"How many CPA's do you know with a black belt? Hell, all I ever do in the evening anyway is read or play with the boa or watch TV."

"Ernie—you're on!" She thought for a moment about kissing him, then changed her mind and shook his hand. It seemed much more professional. Having a real comptroller who could protect the school physically as well as financially was more than she'd have ever dared hope for.

Besides, it would be nice to have a man around the house.

Chapter 12

The word-of-mouth publicity was remarkable. After three weeks, the frenzy of the first night had been forgotten and the school was running more successfully than any of them had anticipated. Men who'd never thought of going to a prostitute came to What's Cooking because it was—as some of them wrote on the little comment cards placed in the bedrooms—"just like doing it on a date."

Ernie Hemmingway was there every night. He'd established a budget and—along with cooling down an occasional hothead and supervising the kitchen—handled paychecks, arranged a system whereby customers could charge their orders on Visa or American Express, and was responsible for spot-checking employee performance. The staff felt comfortable with him. They considered him one of the girls.

"He's a lifesaver," said Sonni.

Joanna and Karen agreed. Working a full-time job and running a House was a much more difficult assignment than they'd thought it would be. It wasn't easy to be cheery, sexy, and happy to cook omelettes after a hard day at the office.

"It's not the screwing that wears me out," said Karen. "It's the listening. I think some of those guys would be just as happy if I were a priest or a bartender."

"Don't bet on it," said Ernie, who also advised the girls on investments. He'd already sold Karen a mutual fund. She was delighted and had cut her schedule to three nights a week so that she could wake early enough in the morning to read through the *Wall Street Journal*.

Surprisingly, Andrea had cut her two work days down to one. When Sonni asked her why, she said, "I don't want to talk about it."

"Is it something that someone did?" Sonni asked, concerned.

Andrea shook her head.

"Well?"

"Well, if you really want to know . . . it's Bernard." She looked at the ceiling the way one did to hold back tears.

"Is he ill?"

"No. He's been dieting and playing golf, tennis. He's never looked better."

"Is he . . . mistreating you?"

"He's never been so kind and considerate. He's doing his own laundry and he doesn't hassle me about where I've been or how much money I've spent. He even bought me a lynx coat."

"So?"

"SO?" Andrea's eyes flashed angrily. "Do you think I'm blind?"

"I don't understand."

"Of course you don't. You haven't been married for fourteen years to a man who never remembers a birthday, who asks for tax receipts when he buys popcorn, who wouldn't pick up a dirty sock if it were covering a Krugerand. Don't you see?"

"See what?"

"He's . . . he's having an affair." Andrea began to cry. "I—I don't understand how he could do this to me after fourteen years of marriage."

"Now, wait a minute," Sonni said. She handed Andrea a Kleenex. "In the first place, you're not certain he's having an affair. In the second, well, you've had a few . . . holidays from the marriage yourself." Sonni thought she'd put it well.

"Christ, can you blame me? Being married to a man who putts after sex, never reads a single poem I write, who's so absorbed in cataclysm that he doesn't even see the disaster he's made of our marriage? My affairs have kept us together. I mean, God knows I'm entitled to *some* pleasure. What does *he* have to cheat for?" Andrea's self-image had always been unshakable.

Sonni was thoroughly confused. "I never realized you felt that way about Bernard; but if he's that bad, why are you cutting out a working night to be at home?"

"Well, he's not going to feel guilty if I'm not there, is he?"

"But if you don't care about hi—"

"I never said I didn't *care*," Andrea said indignantly. "After fourteen years of marriage a woman cares. For all I know, my suddenly having a career might be responsible.

He might feel threatened by having a working wife." Bernard believed Andrea was a night instructor at a culinary institute. "Maybe I've pushed him into a midlife crisis, in which case he needs me. He's never been very good in crises, you know." Her eyes softened, misted for a moment, then slowly narrowed to two icy hyphens. "But if that's not the case, if he's just having an affair for a change of nookie, then he's going to pay for it. And pay plenty. I'm going to take half of every breath he takes for the rest of his life."

On a strictly business level, Sonni could see why Andrea wanted to spend Wednesday nights at home.

Evelyn, on the other hand, after recovering from her first-night jitters and Ernie's karate chop, had signed on full time. In fact, she'd become a workaholic.

There was no longer any doubt about what had made Evelyn Stang the Mostess Hostess at Camp Lettingo. She handled more orders on a given night than most women did in a month. Her stamina was awesome. Blonde, brunette, or redhead, she would still draw two or three of her customers back for seconds the same night. She was delighted with her income; she'd already saved enough for a vacation next month at Club Med, where, she said, "I just want to lay on my back and not think of work."

Sonni was at the school every night to see that all ran smoothly, which it usually did. And which was more than she could say for the rest of her life.

Her father and Flossie were going to marry. And on the same day that Irv Mishkin asked Sonni to arrange the reception, Albie Drury informed her that he wanted George Wilkins out of the wheelchair and expected Sonni to arrange the miracle.

The toeless weatherman was to rise and walk the day before Thanksgiving. Albie had wanted to wait till Christmas—the season for miracles—but Wilkins wasn't willing to sit still that long. After his first week on the air, his fan mail was double that received by any member of the news team. Not only were his forecasts accurate—so accurate that he could predict showers to the hour in any five-day forecast—but his wheelchair delivery came across with such verisimilitude that viewers wrote of being inspired by his courage. Lately he'd taken to telling brave little jokes about being a paraplegic, about how he never had to worry about *standing* in the rain or *running* for a taxi. Sonni felt he was carrying it too far, but Albie loved it, and, according to the surveys, George Wilkins was the biggest draw on the *Nightly News*. The problem was, he knew it.

Just to taunt Albie, Wilkins would sometimes spring out of his chair while off camera and do a pelvic-swinging pantomime of Elvis Presley, then scoot back mere moments before his cue. While upstairs knew nothing about Wilkins' ambulatory abilities, the rest of the staff did. It was one of the best-kept secrets in the news business.

It was also one of the most difficult. Once Wilkins realized he had media clout, he began making demands. He demanded a room where he could work out before the show.

"I don't like sittin' around on my ass all day," he told Albie.

"What do you think you're getting paid for?"

"I'm supposed to be getting paid for tellin' folks if they should wash their car or take that picnic, not for busting my butt in this thing." He scowled at Albie. "I bet you wouldn't ask a white man to do it."

"If he were a paraplegic and a good weatherman, I certainly would."

"Bullshit!" said Wilkins.

Albie arranged to have a set of barbells and a Jog-o-matic treadmill brought into the file room between 2 and 3 P.M., when the room could be locked and Wilkins would be able to work out without fear of detection. He also hired a masseuse to give Wilkins a back rub before the show. She was a frowzy anorexic from a local massage parlor called Venus's Flytrap, and Albie had to pay her plenty to keep her mouth shut.

"We've got to get that sonofabitch on his feet soon," Albie told Sonni.

"You said Thanksgiving," she reminded him.

"I'm tempted to up it to Columbus Day."

"A miracle on Columbus Day?" Sonni made a face. "It'll lose something."

"All right, all right. I'll wait, But it better be worth waiting for. I want it set up right. You know what I mean?"

Sonni knew what he meant. Albie wanted Wilkins to reminisce at least three times a week on how it had been when he could walk; to talk about what he'd felt when he used to climb the old apple tree, and then break off mid-sentence, sock his fist into his hand, and deliberately change the subject. Albie wanted the viewers to feel for Wilkins, to pray for him. "The bottom line," he said, "is that the best miracles are the ones that answer prayers."

He wanted nothing but the best on the *Nightly News*.

The plan was thoroughly repugnant to Sonni—but Albie was beyond moral reasoning, and her expenses were still beyond her draw from the school. She told Albie not to worry, that she'd take care of everything, knowing full well that the real miracle would be to stop her father from marrying Flossie Gerber.

Sonni was annoyed that she had to meet her father at an Off-Track Betting parlor, but it was one of the few places he went without Flossie these days.

"Are you really sure you want to do this?" she asked.

"Would I ask you to make me a wedding reception if I wasn't?" He'd just explained that he wanted a small affair at Tower in the Park, a high-rise catering hall in Queens that was known for its weddings, bar mitzvahs, and chopped-liver swans. Irv wanted a swan circled by a Dinky.

"It's not that." She looked around, as if to find someone who might help her, and saw that she was the only woman in a room filled with men. She felt outnumbered. "Look, Daddy, this isn't where we should be discussing this."

"What's to discuss? I've told you everything." He lit an expensive cigar, a panatela.

"I thought you'd switched to those red cigarettes."

"Well . . . only for Flossie. They make her happy. But this is sort of an occasion. I thought I'd treat myself. I haven't had one of these in years." He excused himself, puffing proudly, and went to the window to place a bet; he had a tip from his superintendent on Zuki's Cookies in the third. He returned holding a ten-dollar win ticket.

"At ninety to one, I figure this could pay for our honeymoon," he said.

"Dad, listen—"

"Oh, I forgot to mention. Flossie said be sure to send invitations to the governor, the mayor, and the President."

Sonni blinked. It bothered her to be even fleetingly impressed. "How does she know them?"

"She doesn't. But she told me that she invited them to

her last wedding, and the governor and his wife sent a candy dish with their regrets."

"That's disgusting."

"What's disgusting? It was crystal." He shrugged. "Maybe not the best . . ."

"You know what I mean. Dammit, Daddy, I don't know how to say this, but—" She was jostled by a man reading a racing form as he walked toward a window.

He said, "I beg your pardon. I—" he stopped, and cocked his head to the side. "Well, well, well. Hellooo." It came out like a wolf whistle.

Sonni flushed. She recalled helping the wolf-whistler with a mushroom omelette about a week ago. She would either have to acknowledge him or pretend he'd mistaken her for someone else. Then again, a brief nod might just send him on his way. She tried the brief nod and turned back to her father.

It didn't work.

The wolf-whistler, who wore a star sapphire pinky ring and two gold chains and looked like the indolent scion of a ladies' coat and suit firm that had fallen on hard times, eased himself next to Sonni. "I didn't know you had take-out orders," he said.

"I'm afraid you're mistaking me for someone else." She said it as icily and virginally as she could. This was neither the time nor the place to tell her father about her business.

"Hey, grimme a break." He glanced at Irv and back to her. "I wasn't born yesterday, sugar." He ran his hand along Sonni's arm. "I'm not in a hurry. When you're through with him, I'm right around the corner on Fifty-third."

Damn! As if she needed a business problem on top of

everything else right now. Before she could say anything, Irv Mishkin tapped the wolf-whistler on the shoulder.

"My name's Mishkin," he said.

The wolf-whistler turned, slightly flustered. "Oh . . . uh, Smith." He extended his hand.

Irv Mishkin took the cigar from his mouth and extinguished it in Smith's palm.

Sonni was dumbfounded. Her father had never done anything like that.

"Let's go," he said, remarkably calm considering Smith's scream.

They hurried out to the street and then into a coffee shop, where Irv found two seats at the end of the counter.

"You have to know how to handle punks, Son. Decisive action is the only thing they understand."

Sonni felt that Smith might have understood a firm rebuff just as well, but remained silent. When Irv Mishkin sacrificed a panatela, you didn't want to tell him it had been unnecessary.

Irv ordered two egg creams. "So," he said, "as you were saying?"

Sonni fiddled with her napkin. "I was saying that . . . well, I don't think you're doing the right thing."

"You don't like the Tower In the Park? It's where the old World's Fair was. They have a terrific view. You can see Kennedy Airport—"

"It's not the reception I'm talking about. It's the marriage."

"You can't have one without the other."

"Have you considered forgoing both?"

The egg creams arrived. Irv sipped his slowly. "Flossie

told me I should expect this," he said quietly. "But I guess I just didn't expect it."

"Flossie told you to expect what?"

"That you'd object. She told me it was natural. Believe it or not, it's happened to her before."

Sonni believed it.

"Her last two husbands had children, and both times the kids tried to prevent the marriage. She explained it to me. There's some psychological term for why they didn't want her to take their mother's place."

"Intelligence," Sonni whispered to herself. "Look, Daddy, I have nothing against stepmothers, I just think you're . . . well, you're taking the wrong step."

"How can you say that? The woman has been working day and night to get my Dinky off the ground. She handles the phone calls, the letters, the orders . . ."

"What orders?"

"Well . . ." Irv took another sip of his egg cream. "These things take time."

"Maybe you're right," Sonni said grudgingly. "But I still think she's using you as a meal ticket."

"Meal ticket—me? She does all the cooking. She treats me like a prince. Okay, so maybe not all the time, but even princes don't want to be treated like princes *all* the time. And she does pamper me. She doesn't even want me to get up to answer the phone. I'm telling you, she's as selfless as the day is long."

Sonni pointed out that the days were getting shorter.

"Son, Son." Irv Mishkin took her hand in his, sighed. "You've still got a lot to learn about certain women."

Sonni didn't have the heart to tell him that where certain women were concerned, some things were better not to know.

Sonni was depressed walking back to the office. She hadn't managed to reach her father at all. Before Flossie, Irv had not only sought Sonni's advice but followed it. Oh, there were times when he'd been stubborn, decided to act like a parent and do things his way just to feel independent; but he'd usually discover that Sonni was right before any real damage was done. By the time he'd realize this mistake, it would be too late. Flossie didn't believe in divorce for any woman over fifty who had an income under six figures, and Irv Mishkin wasn't homicidally inclined.

Then again, Sonni thought, maybe it wasn't her father who was making the mistake. Maybe she was. So the woman exaggerated. If she wanted people to believe that her son's tonsilectomy had been as complicated as a coronary bypass, that her gallstones had been as large as tennis balls, so what? If Irv could endure her suffering, why should Sonni care? Everyone had some redeeming feature. Flossie couldn't be all *that* bad.

Sonni changed her mind five minutes later.

In the window of a novelty shop on Broadway, she spotted a life-sized inflatable plastic doll. It was very pink and completely naked, though half hidden from view by a large poster that said: "Suzy *never* has a headache."

The blatant sexism appalled her. But she was more disturbed by the thought that the doll, at least theoretically, was competition. Though Suzy couldn't respond, she couldn't complain either; and from what Sonni had learned about men, there were many who didn't mind the trade-off. She moved closer for a better look, and was heartened by Suzy's irregular seams.

Then she saw the shelf with the glasses: six of them, tall, frosted, and ringed with a daisy chain of lemons. The sign beside them said: "FLO'S WONDERADE. NO CALORIES. JUST ADD WATER. REUSABLE. $10.00."

They had to be Flossie's. But how . . ? Of course! The
truth came to Sonni like a slap. Flossie had used for herself
the three thousand that was to promote the Dinky.

How could her father be so blind? No wonder the Dinky wasn't selling. His goddam Gerber Baby, his *special*
woman, had taken him to the cleaners before she'd even
gotten him to the altar.

Sonni went inside. Ten dollars was a hell of a lot cheaper than a reception at Tower In The Park. Tucking the
box of glasses under her arm gave her a lot more faith in
miracles.

Chapter 13

Sonni relaxed. There were few things more satisfying than having first impressions justified. The lemonade glasses were irrefutable evidence that her feeling about Flossie hadn't been just sour grapes. When her father phoned the next day, she chatted amiably, remained amiable even after Flossie picked up the extension to say that she'd found the best dressmaker in New York for her gown and that her son Seymour was sending a case of ginseng for the wedding. It was easy for Sonni to be gracious; she held the trumps.

How she would play them was another matter.

To confront Flossie at Irv's apartment was tempting, but it had drawbacks: it was a rotten thing to do. There was no need to unnecessarily hurt her father. A private little get-together with Flossie would be much more effective. If it worked out, the Gerber Baby would have an inexplicable change of heart and vanish from Irv's life like a small stain in the wash—especially if Sonni didn't try to wring her for the three thousand.

Sonni invited Flossie to lunch at the Russian Tea Room. It seemed fitting to have a confrontation over borscht. Sonni had read somewhere that it was what the workers gulped down before they overthrew the czar.

"Well," Flossie said, raising her glass, "to my new daughter to be."

"Whoever she *may* be," said Sonni, and clinked. She took a long swallow of her Bloody Mary. When she looked up, Flossie was slowly lowering her untouched whiskey sour to the table. Her eyes were narrowed; a Siberian husky on alert.

"What's that 'whoever she may be' supposed to mean?"

"That *she* is not going to be *me*."

Flossie broke off a piece of pumpernickel and smeared it with butter, nodding as she did. "Oh?"

"Oh."

Flossie took a large bite, began to chew slowly. "I see," she said, without the slightest perturbation.

"I don't think you do," said Sonni. "What I'm telling you is that you're not going to marry my father."

"Since when have you become an oracle?"

"It isn't a prediction, it's an ultimatum."

'An ultimatum, no less." Flossie took another piece of bread. "Have you told this to your father?"

"I haven't told anything to my father. Yet. But I will if I have to."

"I guess you'll have to," Flossie said sweetly, "because I'm just going to pretend I didn't hear you. I've been

threatened before. Mel's Kids tried to send me a letter
bomb." She chucked Sonni under the chin. "I'll tell you
something, Miss Ultimatum, your father's going to marry
me whether you like it or not. And you know why? Because he likes what he's getting and the way that I'm giving it." She laughed—a throaty, despotic laugh, a laugh
Sonni could imagine coming from the czar after a po-
grom.

The waiter brought the borscht. Sonni watched as Flossie spooned a hefty dollop of sour cream into her bowl and
mashed it into the soup.

Sonni stared at her own bowl, took one sip, then put
down her spoon. "Why is my father's Dinky not being
marketed—" she pulled a Wonderade glass from her
purse—"and these are?"

Flossie blanched, turned the color of the sour cream
floating in her soup. She opened her mouth, but Sonni
didn't give her a chance to say anything.

"You took the money I gave my father for the Dinky,
lied to him, and used it yourself. For these."

Flossie was still for a moment, then she picked up her
spoon. "Big deal."

"Big deal!" Sonni stared in amazement. "You steal from
a man who trusts you, lie to him, cheat him out of a
dream, and all you can say is 'Big deal'?"

"What do you want, the pledge of allegiance?"

"I want you to tell him that you can't marry him, and
then disappear."

"Or?"

"Or I'll tell him everything and take you to court for
the three thousand dollars."

Flossie took a spoonful of borscht. "I'll need a little
time. You wouldn't want me to break off with him just
like that."

"Wouldn't I?"

"He's no spring chicken, you know. A sudden shock could . . ." Flossie let her voice trail off and licked some sour cream from her spoon.

"All right," Sonni said quickly, not wanting to deal with the implication. "Two weeks."

"That's only fourteen days."

"Mount Everest was scaled in less." Sonni signaled the waiter.

He came over and looked quizzically at the table. "Are you through?" he asked.

"Definitely!" Sonni requested the check and left, lavishly tipping the confused waiter.

Escaping oppression was worth any price.

After three months, What's Cooking was running well in the black. Many nights there were more customers than the staff could handle comfortably, especially Wednesdays, when Andrea's absence was noticeably felt by all. Sonni had hired two of Evelyn's friends on a part-time basis out of necessity. They were United Airlines stewardesses and had New York layovers twice a week.

Lately many of the customers were from out of town. One Friday night there was a computer software salesman from Detroit, an aeronautics engineer from Houston, an antique dealer from Cincinnati, and two authors on tour for their books (*The Layman's Guide to Alternate Realities* and *The Joy of Drooling: An Illustrated Handbook for Dieters*). They'd heard about the place from friends. Arthur Fletcher, a wealthy Los Angeles impresario who managed a string of celebrity impersonators, had become a regular; he'd heard about the place from three of his Mormon Tabernacle Choir look-alikes. Sonni was thrilled that What's Cooking was getting such a good reputation.

But she didn't know *how* good until she received a letter from a woman she didn't know and an organization she'd never heard of.

The letter arrived on a Thursday, postmarked Chicago. It was from the president of WOLVERINE. It said:

> *You must be doing something right. We'd like to know*
> *what it is. Keeping the faith, in the life,*
> BELLE CORDAY

"What's WOLVERINE?" Sonni handed Ernie the letter. "And who's Belle Corday?"

"She's a well-known Chicago madam," he said, petting Mouse, who lay quiet and motionless in his lap. "WOLVERINE is the organization she founded: Women of Leisure Voluntarily Earning Rightful Income Nightly, Enjoyably."

"How do you know that?"

"I've been around." He put Mouse in his out basket and leaned back, put his feet up on the desk.

Sonni looked at him curiously. She'd come to know him fairly well, trusted him as an accountant and adviser, but there was still a lot about Hemmingway the man that remained a mystery to her.

"How did she hear about us?" Sonni asked.

He shrugged. "Men talk. Someone—or several someones—most likely came here and then went back and told her that her place didn't stack up against yours."

"That's rude." Sonni was ashamed that one of her customers would do something like that.

"Rude but true. I've been to Corday's. It's just a House.

This place is like a home. It's got warmth, atmosphere. There's something special about getting laid and smelling eggs cooking in the kitchen. A lot more men would pay for sex if all brothels were like this."

Sonni gripped his shoulder. "That's it!"

"Huh?"

"Ernie, it's time."

He looked at his watch. "For what?"

"To unfurl, to stretch, to broaden our horizons; to bring moderate-priced quality sex to men who thought they had to come to New York to get it." She took a deep breath. "Ernie, we're going to expand."

"Expand? You keep telling me you hardly have enough time for this place."

"That's true, but it can be done." Her eyes glinted excitedly.

"How?"

"Think, Ernie. Think big. Think *really* big. What comes to mind?"

"Mastodon?"

"*Franchise!* Don't you see, Ernie, we can franchise."

"Sonofabitch. You are a genius." He looked at her with unconcealed admiration. "What a woman."

Sonni flushed, immensely pleased with Ernie's response and enormously impressed with herself. She'd always thought the Red Sox were an underrated team.

"By God," he said, "do you realize it could be the perfect answer for every man who has to go on the road?"

Sonni didn't realize it; she told him to continue.

"Look, when you're in a strange city and want clean dependable lodging, where do you go?"

"Um . . . a Howard Johnson's."

"Right. Or a Mariott, a Hilton, a name-brand place

where you're confident that certain standards will be met, where there won't be unpleasant surprises."

"I once found a pair of dirty socks in a drawer at the Hilton."

"What I mean is that if you're at a Holiday Inn in Mozambique, it's no different than being at one in Secaucus."

"Do they have one in Secaucus?"

"That's not the point. Listen, when a man's in a strange city and wants to get laid, he's got problems. Sure, a night clerk can fix him up, but that's risky. Most guys just forget about it and sit in their hotel room and watch soft-core on the tube. But if they knew of a House where they could count on safe, affordable, satisfying sex, a name-brand brothel, they'd be there."

Sonni's excitement soared. "Especially if they could find it easily—in the Yellow Pages under 'Cooking Schools.' "

"You've got it!"

Sonni leaned back against the wall; stared. Never in her niche-searching fantasies had she envisioned owning a chain of name-brand brothels. "I can lease the name, the menu, the five-minute foreplay formula; set the standards for the girls and—"

"And for the décor," Ernie said.

"The décor?"

"Absolutely. Think of McDonald's golden arch. Familiarity breeds success. All the franchise schools must have baseball bats, Asian artifacts, a cat, and five omelettes."

"You're right." Sonni socked her palm. "Damn. I wish I could start right away."

"Why can't you?"

"I have problems being in three places at the same

time." Aside from the school, there was still her father and a miracle to take care of. "Damn. The timing is so right. What can I do?"

"Well . . . you could leave it to me."

"Would you be able to do it?"

"With pleasure," he said.

The following day Ernie resigned from WCBN and became a full-time franchise salesman. He flew to six major cities and prepared a feasibility study giving a traffic count of various location possibilities—average income of the area, number of target prospects available, morals laws, police corruptibility, and other factors critical to success. When he returned he drew up a financial report that could be shown to prospective franchisees and asked Sonni to put together a complete operating manual on all phases of the operation, and to be sure to include profiles of best customers by age, occupation, and income.

"Why's that necessary?" Sonni asked, removing Mouse from atop Ernie's desk so that she could see his notes.

"The rule is: twenty percent of your customers account for eighty percent of your business."

"I never looked at it that way before."

"Once we start franchising, you'll never look at it another way again." He took out a small black notebook. "Okay. We still have a couple of things to clear up. First, I think your best bet will be to use a canned training program.

"What's that?"

"A film or videotape of what we do and how we do it, the whole menu from soup to nuts—or rather, from foreplay to omelettes. It's a—"

"Whoa! Forget it."

"Forget what?"

"Franchising is one thing, but I'm not making dirty movies."

"It's a *training* film."

Sonni folded her arms. "And wouldn't the boys in the service love to see it. Uh-uh."

"Listen. The whole point of a franchise is that the franchisee cashes in on expertise and doesn't have to obtain it through trial and error. Sure, we're offering them sort of a trademark that has already gained public acceptance in exchange for a share of their profits, but we also have to provide training and a consulting service on a continuing basis. A canned program is a lot easier and less expensive than sending out individual trainers."

"But the operating manual I'm preparing will be complete."

"One picture is worth a thousand words."

Sonni shook her head. "I don't know."

"Think ahead. If we go international, employees who can't even read can be trained instantly."

"I suppose you're right. It just seems a little . . . unsavory."

"It's thoroughly professional. Big businesses do it all the time. And if the franchisee keeps the tape, that eliminates the need for refresher courses."

Ernie had a point. If she preferred modesty to profit, she was in the wrong field. "Okay," she said.

"Good." Ernie made a small check in the black book. "Now, do you think we should set a monthly customer quota?"

"No. We're not supplying product. But we should set mandatory working hours, and I do want weekly reports."

"Okay. Then that's about it." He closed the book.

"What happens now?" Sonni asked.

"Leave it to me," Ernie said.

And, once again, Sonni did.

A week later, at a Holiday Inn in Chicago, Ernie met with Belle Corday and a number of other WOLVERINE members from various parts of the country.

"How's it going?" Sonni asked when he phoned.

"Belle Corday's What's Cooking should be ready for business in less than a month."

"Great! What about the others?"

"We'll see. I'm still laying the groundwork."

Two weeks before Thanksgiving, Ernie returned exhausted but with contracts in hand. He flew back to Chicago with Sonni for the opening of the first franchise.

"Hi, What's Cooking? We're here to serve you," Belle Corday said warmly when she greeted them at the door. "Come on in and make yourself at home."

Ernie made introductions.

"Pleased to meet you," Belle said, "and I'm proud to be part of the team." She winked at Sonni. "That's some great training film. I'm thinking of showing it every night, you know, just to sort of get the girls going."

Sonni blushed. "I'm glad you find it helpful."

The president of WOLVERINE looked nothing like what Sonni had expected. She was short and frail, delicately birdlike in her motions, with a high forehead and skin the color of skim milk. Soft-spoken, she was dressed all in black and could easily have been taken for a nun, were it not for the fact that she repeatedly referred to her customers as fuck-happy cocksuckers.

Sonni made a note to have Ernie talk to her about that.

The apartment, a Lakeshore Drive condominium, was more or less a duplicate of Ta'Shi Palmetto's, right down to the bats in the kitchen and the litter box in the bathroom.

Sonni congratulated Ernie. "Remarkable," she said.

"It's only the beginning," he replied.

The following week they flew to San Francisco. In the heart of Chinatown a buxom sable-haired Eurasian madam named Lotus showed Sonni around rooms identical to those she'd seen in Chicago. The greatest difference between the San Francisco What's Cooking and the other two was that the menu was printed in English and Chinese. Ernie told Sonni, when they left, that he felt they scrimped a bit on foreplay but made up for it with pelvic enthusiasm and terrific stir-fried omelettes.

That night, on a virtually empty 747, Sonni discussed revamping the menu.

"I think we could make the Handyman's Delight more popular by promoting it as "no-muss no-fuss gratification for the man in a hurry." She pulled a long typewritten report from her attaché case.

"What's that?" he asked.

"Belle's first-week comment sheet. Look at this: 'Handyman's Delight most requested by 18–25-year-olds. One girl can serve four in an hour.' At twenty-five bucks a Delight, that can be very profitable."

"Hmmm," Ernie said. "We haven't had many orders for them in New York. I mean, even at twenty-five dollars, a hand job is still just a hand job."

"That's the point. We've got to make our hand jobs *special*. Different. You have to admit that if we can come up with a unique hand job, we've got a real winner." She thrummed her fingers on the attaché case, thought for a moment, then took her hairbrush from her purse and began running her palm up and down the handle. "There has to be a better way to stroke a penis."

"Don't you ever forget about work?" Ernie yawned, leaned against the pillow he'd propped by the window, and closed his eyes.

"I wish I could." It seemed she was always thinking of work. Sometimes she even thought about why she *wasn't* thinking about it. She gripped the brush with her left hand and played her fingers against the handle as if it were a piccolo, as if she were playing "The Flight of the Bumblebee." It was interesting, different. It might work.

Somewhere over Kansas she tried it out on Ernie.

"It's a winner," he said, then zipped up and went to sleep.

Sonni drew a rough schematic diagram of the movements. She'd send copies to Chicago and San Francisco in the morning; a revised Handyman's Delight would be profitable, but it wasn't worth shooting a supplemental training film for. She settled back, feeling entitled to relax. She picked up the airline magazine and began to work the crossword puzzle.

The message light on her answering machine was lit. It cheered her. It was like coming home to someone; a greeting. Living alone had merit, but there were times when she would prefer company. Coming home after a trip was one of those times. She'd invited Ernie to stop up for coffee, but he had to pick up a mouse for his boa.

The machine indicated three messages. Sonni tried to guess who they might be. She guessed her father, Joanna, and Andrea. She was wrong about all three.

The first was from Albie Drury. He sounded upset, as if

he'd been crying or drinking or both. What Sonni gathered from his disjointed sentences was: George Wilkins, disguised in a long Rastafarian wig and dark glasses, had been spotted zipping down Houston Street on a skateboard, and recognized by an outraged politician. It boded ill for the miracle, for Albie's job, and for WCBN, which, for all its shortcomings, was still the only station that broadcast reruns of the World Series. Albie asked Sonni to call him at home as soon as she got in. He repeated his number twice.

The second message was from Flossie Gerber. It was chilling and cryptic. All she said was, "I know what's cooking, cookie."

Sonni's stomach lurched, as if she were in an elevator and had heard a cable snap. As obtuse as Flossie's message was, it was perfectly clear. Somehow she'd found out about the school and was ready to teach Sonni a lesson she wouldn't forget. But before the full implications of that seeped in, the next message began. It was the shortest of them all, and the most upsetting. It only said what was relevant: "Stelson here. Seven fifty-three. Will call back re sex and money."

The elevator that had begun falling with Flossie's message plunged. Sonni switched off the machine. *Stelson.* She couldn't call Albie, couldn't even think about Flossie. All she could think about as she walked into the kitchen was Wyatt Stelson.

"Wyatt Stelson," she said aloud, realizing that it was the first time she'd ever spoken his full name. She was too upset to search for the significance. The bastard. The sonofabitch. Did he think he could just appear quarterly like some poetry journal and be welcomed? And what sort of message was that to leave on a machine? How did he know she hadn't married and that her husband wouldn't hear it? Shouldn't the People's Person care? And if he'd had her number all along, why hadn't he called before? She took out a box of Wheaties and began to munch on them, grinding the flakes into paste with her teeth.

Well, at least she was forewarned and had time to prepare something devastating to say, though when she stopped to think about it what could she say to a man who thought she was a call girl—now that she was one?

It was confusing and very upsetting. Why did she hate the man so much? Why did it matter that she did? She hated lima beans and had never searched for reasons.

But lima beans had never held the promise of a meaningful relationship; had never turned her on only to turn her off. Wyatt Stelson wasn't just lima beans, and she knew it.

She knew it for certain later when, in the middle of her reliable beachboy-gets-fine-lady-executive-in-the-cabana fantasy, the beachboy turned into the People's Person, the cabana turned into her bed, and her vibrator turned back the clock to a night she thought she'd erased from her mind forever.

Chapter 14

"He was on a skateboard, a goddam skateboard!" Albie shouted, pounding a fist on his desk.

"So I understand," Sonni said abstractedly. She was wondering whether Wyatt Stelson had ever been a beach-boy.

"We're dead. Gone. We can all kiss our asses goodbye," he moaned, burying his head in his hands.

"Now, wait a minute." It was time to pay attention. "You told me that Wilkins was wearing a wig. How could this—"

"If your father put on a wig and got on a skateboard, would you know him?"

Sonni could not imagine her father in a wig, let alone on a skateboard. "I'd probably pretend I didn't."

Albie leaned over the desk, his eyes wide. He pointed at

her. "But you'd *know* him. People know faces that they see every day."

"I don't see my father every day." Which reminded her she was supposed to see him that night. She'd made the date before she'd gotten Flossie's phone message.

"But people see Wilkins every day—in their living rooms, their bedrooms. He's part of their family. They know his face as well as their own."

"But this guy who saw him, allegedly saw him, has no proof that it was Wilkins."

"Proof? Proof? The guy's a politician. He doesn't need proof. He's after publicity. All he has to do is investigate. He doesn't care if it was or wasn't Wilkins on that skateboard. The trouble is that the asshole is going to luck into uncovering the sleaziest hoax in TV history. We're dead, I'm telling you. We're dead." Albie made small choking noises and turned to face the window.

Sonni didn't have the heart to tell him that she was planning to quit right after Thanksgiving anyway. It would be too cruel; it would be like buying a skateboard for a paraplegic.

"Who is this politician?" Sonni asked.

"I don't know. I never heard of him," Albie snapped. His head was down and he was fingering the Venetian blinds like a sulky child. "His name is Sucks or Spitz or something like that. Spitz, I think. Yeah, he kept repeating it like he was making some sort of campaign speech." He turned back to Sonni and pursed his lips. "Bill Spitz knows whence he speaks," he mimicked.

Sonni gaped. "*Bill* Spitz?"

"You know him?"

"He used to be my doorman."

Albie made a face. "Must be someone else. This guy's talking about the Presidency."

"So did my doorman."

Albie eyed Sonni. "You're serious? You think this Spitz is that Spitz?"

"I'd go as far as to say I'm sure of it." She smiled like a mother who had just solved her child's problem.

Albie brightened, but only for a moment. "So what the hell difference if he's your Spitz or any Spitz? He's out to burn our asses."

"He never used to be vindictive." Sonni tried to recall what he was like when he was awake.

"Come on. He was a doorman. Now he wants the Presidency. He's going to use the Wilkins thing as a stepping-stone."

"Then there's only one thing to do," Sonni said calmly. "Kill him."

"My God!"

"Just a thought."

"Jeezus, Sonni, this is no time for jokes."

"The whole thing is a joke. Hiring Wilkins in the first place was a joke. A news show with a quota on murders, rapes, and cancer scares is a joke." She heard her voice rising. "The only honest thing about the *Nightly News* is the race results on Thursday nights, but they're fixed before they get here, before they're even run. On a morality level, our show makes Jack the Ripper look like Christiaan Barnard. The only time we ever cover congressional activities is if there's a scandal; the only time we ever cover urban problems is if somebody has died, could die, or will die. We were the only news show last Easter to give a half minute to the Pope and eight minutes to the egg hunt at the Playboy Mansion."

Albie ran his hand through his hair, rolling his eyes upward. "Christ. The last thing I need now is a serious lecture."

"You said you didn't want jokes," Sonni reminded him.

"All I want is my job."

"Then Wilkins walks tonight. We can't wait." Her decisiveness surprised her.

"Tonight? But—but he hasn't rehearsed or anything."

"We don't have a choice."

Albie covered his eyes with his hand. "He's going to blow the whole thing, I just know it."

"He might and he might not," Sonni said, feeling very philosophical.

"It'll be a goddam miracle if he can bring it off," muttered Albie.

"Well," she said, "that's exactly what we want, isn't it?"

The last thing Sonni wanted was to have to deal with Flossie, but there was no way around it, or her. Flossie was sitting behind Sonni's desk when she returned to her office.

"How did you get in?"

Flossie smiled. She was wearing a sheer blouse through which one could see the stalwart stitching of her pink brassiere. Two Bloomingdale's shopping bags were beside her.

"I told the receptionist I was your mother and that I had a surprise for you."

"That's a cheap trick, but you're good at those."

Flossie waved her finger. "I wouldn't be talking about cheap tricks if I were you."

Sonni's palms grew cold. "What's that supposed to mean?" she said, knowing quite well.

"It means, dear child, that I know all about your little

omelette bordello." Flossie pronounced it "board-e-low,"
but Sonni drew small comfort from it. She wondered how
Flossie had found out, but refused to question her.

"What do you want?" Sonni asked stonily.

"Nothing much." Flossie opened her compact and
licked some lipstick from her teeth. "Just your father
and . . . hmmm, twenty-five percent of the action."

"Fuck off!"

"No."

"What do you mean, no?"

Flossie shrugged. "No. I won't fuck off."

Sonni grabbed Flossie's purse and hurled it out the
door. "Then *fetch*."

Flossie sighed tiredly. "That was a very childish thing
to do, but it doesn't faze me. My last daughter-in-law did
much more childish things. She crayoned my reading
glasses, spilled ink on—"

"I'm not your daughter-in-law and I never will be,"
Sonni shouted. "Now get out."

Flossie skinned back her lips and bared her teeth; there
was still a bit of lipstick on them. "Listen, the shoe is on
the other foot this time, tootsie. I'm not moving."

"If you're not out of here in two minutes, I—I'll—"
Sonni hesitated, thought for a moment. "I'll have the police throw you out." If she'd thought longer, she'd probably never have said it.

"Ha!" Flossie snorted. "I'd like to see that."

Half an hour later she did.

As one policeman took down Sonni's complaint, the
other reached politely for Flossie's arm. She swatted him
with her shopping bag.

"Don't touch me. *She's* the prostitute!"

Sonni drew back. The two cops looked knowingly at

each other. Officer Metzger, the older of the two, patted Sonni's arm reassuringly. "We'll handle it. We bring in two or three of them a day."

"Them?"

Flossie began to rant and struggle to free her arm.

"Bag ladies," Metzger explained. "The city's full of them. No homes, no place to go. They sleep in public toilets."

"Public toilets!" Flossie shrieked. "I'll have you know—"

"Calm down, lady," said the officer holding Flossie's arm.

Metzger shook his head. "You're lucky," he said to Sonni. "This one smells a lot better than some of the others. We had one last week: remember, Phil?" He turned to his partner.

Phil, keeping a good grip on Flossie's arm, held his nose. "You mean the Princess?"

Metzger chuckled and nodded. "I'm telling ya," he said, "we didn't even want to put her in the squad car. Stink City! And there she was, carrying on that she's a princess and has diplomatic immunity."

Phil made a face. "She had a lot of things, but I don't think diplomatic immunity was one of them."

"I have identification," Flossie shouted. "It's in my purse. It—it's down the hall, she threw it there."

"Sure," Phil said quietly. "We'll find it." To Sonni he said, "Sometimes they don't even have birth certificates."

Flossie began to redden, rage puffing her cheeks. "I have a Visa card . . . an internist . . . my son's a vegetarian nutritionist." She glared at Sonni. "*She* knows who I am. I sleep with her father."

"Hey," Metzger said, "watch what you say in front of the young lady."

"Young lady, my ass," Flossie snarled. "She's nothing but a whore. She screws guys and makes them omelettes . . . someplace on Park Avenue."

Metzger apologized to Sonni. "I'm really sorry you have to be exposed to all this. If it makes you feel any better, we picked up one once who hurled excrement."

Sonni said it made her feel better.

"Would you stop all this and tell them who I am?" Flossie demanded. "It's gone far enough."

Sonni shrugged helplessly at Metzger. "I never saw her before in my life."

Metzger and Phil pinned Flossie between them and led her out. She spewed curses mightily, but Sonni deflected them. She felt triumphant and almost lightheaded with her lack of remorse until Flossie's final imprecation. It was unexpected and primally lethal; it was like a rabbit punch from God.

"Wait until your father hears about this!"

Mr. Van Danner phoned after lunch to find out why the police had been in Sonni's office. He'd heard about the incident from his secretary, Martha Harrington, the closest thing to a CIA agent WCBN had. Because of her boss's hearing impediment, she was known as "Van Danner's ears."

Sonni told Mr. Van Danner that a bag lady had wandered into her office.

"How did a fag parade get into the building?" demanded Van Danner, who'd obviously not turned up the volume on his telephone.

"Bag lady," Sonni shouted, wondering how he'd turned that into fag parade, though not surprised. Van Danner was phobic about homosexuality; held it responsible for America's decline. Anything more than a firm handshake and a slap on the back between two men was suspect. He spoke avidly against foreign movies, Calvin Klein clothes, and Perrier water, and was disturbed by the celebratory physical contact of the Pittsburgh Steelers. Bowling, as he'd often say, was *his* game. He read *U.S. News & World Report*, the *Wall Street Journal*, and *Guns and Ammo* regularly, and kept copies of *Playboy* in the executive washroom. His wife, Lorna, was an anti-ERA activist who once ran for district representative on a "Buttons and Bows" ticket.

His son Drew was six foot five and had a Thompson submachine gun tattooed on his right arm; he worked as a hairdresser in Greenwich Village.

"Oh," said Van Danner. "What did she want?"

"Who knows? She walked in by mistake."

"To buy a steak?" Van Danner laughed. "That's a good one. A first for WCBN, I guess." Van Danner liked firsts. He was proud of being the first TV executive to use live actors instead of artists' sketches to dramatize trials, despite the several lawsuits that had ensued. He still talked about being the first on his block to own a television set.

Sonni wondered if he would be happy having the first major hoax in TV news history.

Van Danner ended the conversation by telling her that she'd done the right thing. "But before you call the police next time," he said, "call me first."

It was a shame that whether Bill Spitz blew the whistle or George Wilkins' miracle saved the day, Van Danner would be the last to know.

Sonni looked at her watch and realized she'd better get hold of Wilkins. She rang Tina and asked if she knew where he was.

"Why should I?"

"No reason . . . I just thought you might."

"I might, but I don't. Just because we're both black doesn't mean we keep tabs on each other." Tina added, "I am not my brother's keeper," and hung up. She never let anyone get the last word.

Sonni suddenly remembered that George often worked out between two and three in the file room. It was only a quarter of three, so most likely that's where he was.

She knocked three times, then slapped the door. Albie had devised the signal so that George would know it was okay to open up. The door remained locked.

"George. It's me, Sonni," she called softly. Three knocks and another slap. Nothing.

She checked the corridor to make sure no one was around, then called, "George! For Christ's sake, open up. This is no time for games." She thought she heard a muffled sound. On several occasions, Wilkins had hidden in the file room until minutes before air time just to annoy Albie.

"I mean it, George. We've got to rehearse. You're going to walk tonight."

She put her ear to the door and heard an eerie deep howl, like wind around old rafters.

"George?"

The howl grew louder and less ethereal. "George!" Sonni tugged at the handle, but the door wouldn't give. She ran back to Albie's office.

"Quick," she said breathlessly, holding out her hand to Tina, "the key to the file room."

"Where I come from, we say *please*." Tina kept her eyes on the report she was typing.

"It's George! I think he's locked in there! Hurt!"

Tina sighed, typed a last sentence, and turned her typewriter off. "Now, what would George be doing in the file room?"

Jeezus. Albie had her trained. "You know damn well and so do I. Look, just give me the key, will you?"

Tina held up a ring of keys. "Give me it . . . *what?*" She cocked her head.

"Now!"

Tina clicked her tongue, waved a finger. Sonni lunged for the ring, but Tina was quick.

"Not without the magic word."

"Please," Sonni growled.

"Well, that's better." Tina handed them over.

Sonni was out the door. "Tell Albie to meet me at the file room. *Please.*"

She found the right key, after trying several, and pushed open the door. George Wilkins was on the floor, his eyes closed. A one-hundred-pound barbell lay neatly across his chest; a five-hundred-pound filing cabinet that should have been standing in the corner lay neatly across his legs.

"Oh, my God!" Sonni groaned as she lifted the barbell.

George Wilkins remained silent and motionless.

Albie appeared in the doorway. "What the—" He froze. "Is he . . . ?"

"I—I don't think so," said Sonni, "but we'd better get this cabinet off him fast."

"Damn straight," Wilkins mumbled, his eyes still closed.

"George!" Sonni cried. "Are you all right?"

There was no answer.

"George?"

Wilkins rolled his head to the side. "You talking to me?"

"Thank God," Sonni murmured. "We'll have you out

from under this thing in a minute." She stood. "I'll get a couple of cameramen to help."

Albie stopped her at the door. "No," he whispered harshly.

"*No?*"

"Say wha?" mumbled Wilkins.

"What do you mean, no?" Sonni demanded.

"Look over there." Albie pointed to the Jog-o-Matic in the corner. "We've got to hide it. There's no way to explain it if upstairs asks questions. It'll blow everything, everything." His face darkened to a purplish color.

"You're crazy!" Sonni shook her head in utter disbelief.

"Don't you understand? We're dead if we don't get rid of that thing."

"George could be dead if we don't get rid of *this* thing." She moved to get by, but Albie stepped in front of her.

"It's him or us."

"You are crazy!" She pushed him aside and ran down the hall, calling for help and an ambulance. Within moments she had a crowd following her back to the file room. There was a lot of pushing and shoving.

"What happened?"

"Stand back."

Three technicians lifted the cabinet off Wilkins. Mrs. Glick from the accounting department removed her beaded sweater and put it under his head. Tina had battled her way through the crowd. She looked, and screamed. Someone asked if they should call in the mini-cam crew. Someone else asked for Albie.

Albie and the Jog-o-Matic were nowhere in sight.

Before Sonni could even speculate on where they might

have gone, Albie reappeared, looking relieved and trying not to.

"What did you do with the machine?" she asked quietly.

"I hid it—in the perfect place. The stall for the handicapped in the men's washroom."

He considered this a master stroke of fast thinking, and was pleased with the irony until Sonni returned from the hospital and informed him that George Wilkins had a broken spine.

"You mean . . . ?"

Sonni nodded. "He'll never walk again."

Albie socked his fist into his palm. "My God, we're off the hook. It's a *real* miracle!"

At which point Sonni told him that he was a shit and resigned.

Chapter 15

Irv Mishkin paced his apartment like an expectant father named in a paternity suit.

"You shouldn't have done that, Son," he said, shaking his head sadly. He ran his hand abstractedly over his model Dinky, petting it as one would an old but faithful dog.

"I'm only sorry they couldn't hold her." Sonni poured herself a tall drink. She was in no shape to reason with him or confront Flossie, who was expected at any moment. Irv had sent Flossie out to Zabar's, before Sonni had arrived, to buy pistachio nuts. Irv Mishkin used pistachio nuts the way the Greeks used worry beads, as pacifiers. He used cigars the same way. He was now chewing on one of his pacifiers.

"What did she ever do to you?" He extended his hands,

palms upward; a doctor waiting for the nurse to put on his sterile gloves.

"It's what she did to *you,*" said Sonni.

"To me? She cooked for me, rubbed my back, washed me in the tub like a duck."

"A sitting duck," Sonni mumbled.

"What's that supposed to mean?"

"It means she's been taking you to the cleaners," Sonni snapped.

"What cleaners? I use the Martinizing place downstairs."

"You know what I mean."

"If I knew what you meant, would I be asking you? Do you think your father is that kind of man? Do I go up to people and ask them what I already know? Do I say, 'Excuse me, sir, but am I here?' " He smacked his forehead. "Would somebody please tell me what in hell is going on?"

Evidently Flossie had said nothing yet about What's Cooking. Sonni suspected that she was waiting for a real showdown. Well, if that's what she wanted, then she'd get one that would make *High Noon* look like a tête-à-tête. Sonni was going to beat her to the draw. She pulled a Wonderade glass from her purse.

"What's that?"

"*That,*" Sonni said, "is what Gerber Baby has done to your Dinky." She told him how Flossie had stolen his three thousand, cold-bloodedly lied to him, and put her own glasses on the market; told him that the reason she'd done it was in case the marriage fell through or he kicked off.

For a moment Irv stared at her; then, shakily, he got to his feet and put both hands on her shoulders, gripping them as much for support as for paternal contact. His voice quavered when he spoke.

"Son, what you've just said has hurt me as much as anything has ever hurt me in my life, but . . . I raised you and I know in my *kishkas* that you've always been a lousy liar."

"I love you, Daddy," Sonni said.

"I know. And even my broken heart knows you've told me the truth because you want what's best for me." He squeezed her shoulders. "I'm proud of you, Son."

Then she told him that she was the executive manager of a coast-to-coast franchise of brothels.

Irv Mishkin looked as if he'd been strapped too long in a Nautilus machine. "Brothels?" His face turned the color of his cigar ash, which fell to the floor.

"Brothels."

"As in . . ." He made a fist and pushed it forward twice. Sonni nodded.

"The omelette business was that bad? You couldn't have tried crepes?"

Sonni stood very straight. "There never was an omelette business, Dad. Or a cooking school. That's just a front. Men pay for the sex; the omelettes and cooking lessons are free."

"Oh, Son, Son." Irv lowered his head, turned, covered his eyes with his hand. "I never thought I'd say this, but . . . I'm ashamed of you."

A small school of piranhas started a leisurely lunch in her stomach.

"Flossie rubbing me like a duck and then ripping me off, that hurt," he said. "But this . . . this, after I raised you the way I did . . ."

"Daddy, I—"

"For *free* you give omelettes and cooking lessons?"

"Huh?" Sonni blinked, stared.

"In good restaurants they make you pay even for bread and butter. And you're giving away omelettes and cooking lessons when you have captive—*hungry*—customers right there? What kind of business sense is that? Haven't I been able to teach you anything? Look, I'm not saying you should stick them for four-fifty, but a couple of bucks to cover the cost of the eggs, at least."

Sonni opened her mouth, but couldn't speak.

"So, it's a franchise, huh? That's not bad. How many have you got?"

Sonni swallowed. "Three, and there's a possibility of one opening in Miami next month."

"Small but growing." Irv nodded. "I like that. Miami, eh? There's a lot of competition down there, but I've got friends on Collins Avenue. I'll give 'em the word. You got a good accountant? I mean, Son, if nothing else, you're going to have to learn about tax shelters."

Sonni threw her arms around her father and pressed her head against his chest. "Oh, Daddy, I'm so happy, I—" She started to cry.

"There, there," he said, stroking her hair. Neither of them heard the door open.

"Well," Flossie said, "I thought soap operas were only in the afternoon."

Sonni straightened and took a step away from her father. Irv looked at Flossie and then at his daughter. And then for the first time in all Sonni's memory he said, "Over here, Princess," and hugged her to him.

"Flossie," he said somberly, his voice carrying a resonance Sonni had never known it possessed, "how much do I owe you for the nuts?"

"Irvala—" Flossie came toward him—"what sort of silly question is that?"

Irv stepped back, taking Sonni with him as if they were doing a dance step. "Stay where you are."

Flossie's eyes narrowed. She waved the bag of nuts. "All right, what lies has she been telling you?"

"I've told him the truth," Sonni said stonily. "He knows all about what you've done."

"What have I done? Tried to surprise my future husband with a nice going income on a successful novelty? Is that bad? Irvala—" Flossie reached for Irv, but he took another step back.

"All those things you told me about it taking time to sell the Dinky, they were lies, weren't they?"

"No, they weren't lies, they—"

"You never even *attempted* to market it, did you?"

"Irvala, I wanted to surprise you with enough money to market it right. I knew my glasses would sell, but—"

"You had no faith in my Dinky."

"Well, not enough to—"

"All those weeks you were telling me how much you loved it, how you could feel its potential, you were—were—"

"Being nice!" Flossie shouted angrily. "For Christ's sake, it's just another Hula-Hoop!"

Irv released Sonni, slapped his hands. "So. There it is. The truth is out. And now you can get out, too." He pointed to the door.

Flossie sighed. "I didn't mean that. I meant—"

"Yes you did," Sonni said.

Flossie shook the bag of nuts at Sonni. "Look, you, I was willing to to work this all out reasonably, but you've pushed me further than anyone has ever deserved to be pushed." She stifled a smile. "I think you ought to know the *truth* about your *Princess*, Irv."

"He knows," said Sonni.

"I know," said Irv Mishkin.

"You know she runs a whorehouse?"

"Several," Irv corrected.

"And you're not—not upset?" Flossie looked dumbfounded.

"Why should I be?"

"Why *should* you be? Shit, the girl's not running a Burger King, Irv. She's sleeping with men for money."

Sonni said dryly, "And you wouldn't know about things like that. At least my customers know how much they're going to pay and for what."

"Why, you—" Flossie hurled the bag of pistachio nuts at Sonni. She caught it with ease.

"She wasn't the best shortstop P.S. 192 ever had for nothing," Irv said proudly.

"Well, let's see if her father's as good." Flossie grabbed Irv's cigar humidor from the table and raised it over her head. There was a loud snap. Her shoulders heaved forward. She dropped the humidor and clutched her chest.

Irv froze. "My God, her heart!" Instantly he clasped his hands to his own.

"Not quite," said Sonni, smiling broadly for the first time that day. "Retribution."

Flossie Gerber's indefatigable, double-stitched superlatex pink fortress had finally been breached. "*Retribution?*" she shrieked, still cutching herself. "You call *this* retribution? Mel's mother tried to put a contract out on me, only she'd arranged to meet the hit man in a blasting area and short-circuited his pacemaker. *That's* retribution!

And that's nothing compared to what you'll get from me."

Sonni worried about Flossie's retribution for two days and then forgot about it, which was a mistake. It was as much of a mistake as agreeing to meet Albie Drury for a drink.

They met on neutral territory: a Swedish restaurant on Fifty-third Street. He offered her the olive from his martini. "Peace," he said.

"That's an olive *branch*."

He shrugged and ate the olive himself. "Okay. So you're still angry."

"I'm still angry."

"All right, stay angry. But I'm going to make you an offer you can't refuse."

"Try me," she said.

He offered her a job as WCBN's human-interest reporter. "You'll be part of the anchor team, a regular."

"What about Carla? I thought she handled that."

"De Lucca thinks the show's getting too downbeat. Too many rapes and murders. He wants more stories about cabbies returning wallets with thousands in them, dogs saving people from burning buildings, street gangs cleaning up parks."

"Those things don't happen very often."

"Then we'll make them happen."

"Lots of luck," she said.

"Are you saying no?" He looked stunned.

"Yes."

"But why? Christ, they're the easiest stories to beef up and bullshit through. I don't understand."

"That's why," she said.

When she returned home, another message from Wyatt Stelson was on her machine. It said nothing more than that he'd be in touch. She wondered if that was a sexual reference.

Agitated, she turned on the television. Carla Lampretti was giving the *Nightly News* recap. She was saying that the Ku Klux Klan was thought responsible for sabotaging WCBN weatherman George Wilkins' wheelchair. She added that the indomitable Wilkins would be rolling back on the *Nightly News*, as soon as he was able, in a motorized chair paid for by the contributions of well-wishers. Sonni raised the answering machine's volume and replayed Wyatt's message. There was something comforting about hearing an honest voice, even if it was the voice of a man she hated.

She thought about what to say to Wyatt Stelson when he did finally get in touch. She could be cool ("Stelson? Oh, yes, we met on a plane, or was it a bus?") or callous ("Of course I remember you, trivia is my forte") or cruel ("I hope you're not upset, but I forgot to mention that I have syphillis") or maybe even crass ("I never forget a cock").

She dreamt about him that night and said many things, but not in her wildest dream did she imagine what she actually would say when they met.

What she would say was, "Holy shit!"

And, coincidentally, this was exactly what she said the following night when she came face to face with Flossie's retribution.

"Holy shit!"

"Police," said the tallest of the four uniformed officers in the hall outside What's Cooking.

"Police?" Sonni tried to think quickly, but it was as if

her brain had furred over, gone into hibernation. Died.
"Um . . . is there some trouble?"

"There might be. Unfortunately, if there is—you're in
it." He stepped forward.

"Hold it." She flung out her arms, blocking the doorway; the noble last stand of the guilty. "How do I know
you're real policemen?"

"Well, I suppose we could hit you with our regulation
nightsticks, or shoot you with our department-issued thir-
ty-eights, but I assume that this will be sufficient." He
flipped open his wallet and flashed his ID. "Okay?"

"What about them?" She was desperately stalling for
time, though she had no idea what to do with it. If only
she could signal Ernie. Alert the girls. There were only
three customers, but they had to be out before the cops
came in.

"Hey, come on, Agnelli. She's diddling you," said one
of the others.

"Probably what she does best," said another.

"Lay off, you turkeys, I'll handle this," said Agnelli.
"Now, lady, are you going to invite us in or are we going
to have to use force?"

"Don't tell her that, she might be into it. A lot of them
are."

"Would you shut up, Danziger."

"Where's your search warrant?" Sonni demanded. She
wished she could recall one of those detective shows
where women talked their way out of similar situations.
Damn. Where was Ernie?

"Show her, Briggs." Agnelli nudged the slim mustached
officer on his right.

"Show her what? I don't got it."

"Well, what did you do with it?" Agnelli demanded.

"What did *I* do with it? You had it." Briggs said.

"I gave it to you at the station."

"And I gave it back to you when I went for the pizza slices," said Briggs, his voice rising.

"Christ," muttered Agnelli, "it's still in the car, then. Go get it."

"Why do I always have to go? You go. I got the pizzas."

"And I got the Cokes."

"Yeah. And who paid for them? *Me*. Or don't you remember?"

"How could I forget!" said Agnelli, "It was a historic moment."

The officer alongside Briggs leaned back against the wall. "Can this marriage be saved?" He cocked his head toward Danziger. "Pay attention. We've only been together two years. They've been partners for five."

Briggs was shaking his head at Agnelli. "Nice. Real nice," he said. "Who got you thermal underwear last Christmas when you were freezing your ass off? *And* the watch?"

"And who saved your ass when the captain found out you were getting the stuff free from that guy on Delancey for favors?"

"Would you guys knock it off?" Danziger said. "I hear enough of this at home. I'll go downstairs and get the damn warrant."

"You do that," said Sonni, and she slammed the door, double-latching it from the inside.

Ernie hurried across the living room. "What's going on?"

Sonni pointed at the door. "Police," she whispered. "We have to get everyone out."

"Everyone?"

"I mean the customers."

"Precision, Sonni. Precision is survival."

"Right now speed is survival."

"Agreed, but we can't afford a panic."

"We can't afford a bust either, and we don't have much time."

"Okay, let me think. Karen, Chris and Sheryl are in the kitchen with Fletcher. Evelyn's in room two—" he looked at his watch—"and should be just about finishing up with the jockey. And Joanna—uh-oh, she's just gone into one with What's-His-Name, the shrink who wears those pyramids—"

"Bulgerman? He moves about as fast as a lead couch. We're dead."

"Leave it to me. I'll stash the books and have the guys out in three minutes."

"Three minutes? Ernie, that's impossible."

"Impossible?" A small smile pulled the corner of his mouth. "In Nam I evacuated a whole village in less."

"But—"

"Stay here. Stall them as long as you can. Remember, this is a cooking school and you've got the dirty pots to prove it." He patted her shoulder, then lowered his head, hunched forward, and took off across the living room.

Sonni stared at the door, expecting Agnelli's foot to come crashing through at any moment. Damn, damn, damn. Tears welled in her eyes. It wasn't fear of being arrested that upset her. It wasn't even fear of losing her franchises. It was more basic than either: What would her father say? Unconsciously, she ran through excuses in her mind.

"What in hell is happening?" demanded Joanna. She looked tousled and uncharacteristically flustered as she

hurried toward Sonni. "Has Ernie gone beserk? He busted
into the bedroom, tossed Bulgerman over his shoulder,
then ran out like a maniac."

Before she could answer, Karen, Chris, and Sheryl, followed by Evelyn, erupted from the kitchen.

"My God, is it true?" said Karen. "A gas leak?"

"Why didn't Ernie want us to go with him?" demanded
Chris.

"Why was he carrying Mr. Bulgerman out the fire escape?" asked Evelyn.

"Would you be *quiet?*" Sonni whispered hoarsely. She
pointed toward the door. "They're right out there."

"*Who's* right out there?" Joanna asked, annoyed.

"Police, that's who."

"Really?" Joanna brightened. She began fixing her
hair.

Evelyn gasped. "Oh, no . . . oh, no . . ." She shook
her head slowly at first, then more and more rapidly, until
it looked as if she were having a seizure. "They're not
taking me. I've read what goes on in those women's pris-
ons. The guards are all three-hundred-pound lesbians and
they rape you with sausages if you don't let them do what
they want to you and—"

Sonni clapped her hand over Evelyn's mouth. "Would
you please relax? We run a cooking school, remember
that. A cooking school. We have nothing to worry about,
okay?" She removed her hand.

Evelyn nodded. "Okay." She straightened her skirt and
threw back her shoulders; then fainted.

"No!" Sonni cried.

"Open up!" shouted Agnelli, and rapped heavily on the
door.

"Let me deal with them," Joanna said. "I've had experience."

"What about Evelyn?"

"Well, we don't want her in a bedroom. That might give them the wrong idea. Just prop her up someplace where she'll look inconspicuous."

"Where's an unconscious woman going to look inconspicuous?" Karen asked.

"I know just the place." Sonni ran into the living room, turned on the TV and pushed the couch to face it. "Hurry, bring her here." Karen and Chris helped her position Evelyn as Joanna went for the door.

"Well, well, well. I don't believe it," Joanna cried. "If it isn't the blue devil himself!"

Joanna, hands on hips and shaking her head, was grinning broadly at Officer Agnelli. And Officer Agnelli was grinning back.

"JoJo!" Agnelli said. "Hey, Briggs, do you know who this is? Jo-Jo Holbrook."

"Not the same Jo-Jo Holbrook who's been Siren-of-the-Year for three years straight?"

"The same," said Joanna demurely.

Briggs removed his hat. "Pleased to meet you, ma'am," he said, then awkwardly introduced Danziger and his partner, Stern.

"We met at the precinct New Year's party," said Stern.

"I remember," said Joanna. She winked and he blushed.

"I'm afraid I never had the pleasure," said Danziger, extending his hand.

Joanna shook it. "Well, we'll have to rectify that. Come on in."

Sonni held her breath, but not one of them even glanced at Evelyn. Within minutes, Joanna had made introductions, gotten assurances of protection and taken orders for two His, one Hers, and a Handyman's Delight (this last from Stern, who explained he'd had a full meal at home before going on duty).

As soon as Ernie returned, Sonni would make sure he arranged a bonus for Joanna.

Chapter 16

Briggs and Danziger stood at the counter chopping mushrooms for their omelettes. Stern sat talking to Karen. He looked dazed and surfeited. Agnelli, shirtless except for his bulletproof vest, was wolfing down pieces of cheese.

"He wore it the whole time," Joanna whispered to Sonni, pointing to Agnelli's vest.

"The city's rougher than it used to be," sighed Sonni. For the last hour she'd been cleaning the kitchen, which Ernie's impromptu evacuation had left in chaos. She just wanted to lie down. Alone.

"It was really wonderful," Joanna continued. "I—I think I had an orgasm."

Sonni's head snapped up. "Fantastic! But what do you mean, you *think*?"

"How can I be sure? I never had one before." Joanna paused, frowned. "And if I never have one again, I'll never know if I did."

"That should be your biggest worry."

"It is," said Joanna.

The doorbell rang.

"That must be Ernie." Sonni jingled a key chain. "He dropped these here. I'll get it."

As she left the kitchen, she realized how lucky they were with the way things had turned out. Someone up there must really like omelettes, she thought. She opened the door.

"Holy shit!" she said.

In the doorway, carrying an attaché case and holding the sort of hat worn by English country gentlemen and New York cabbies, was Wyatt Stelson.

"I beg your pardon," he replied. "I—It's *you!*" He stared at her, and she stared back. He was bald as an egg.

Sonni was dumbfounded. "How did you find me?" she asked.

"You opened the door."

"I mean, how did you know I'd be . . . here?"

"I didn't, to be perfectly honest—which I usually am— but it is an interesting coincidence, isn't it?"

Interesting coincidence! Was that his only reaction? Sonni clamped on a sudden urge to kick him in the balls.

"Should I start shooting now, TPP?" Only after he'd spoken did Sonni notice that standing apart from Wyatt was a bearded young man holding a video camera. It was leveled at Sonni.

She drew back instinctively. "Who's *he?*"

"Dustin Levy, my cameraman."

Dustin nodded and brushed past Sonni into the apartment. "Not too much light in here." He began to pan the room.

Sonni whirled and slapped her hand over the lens. "What do you think you're doing?"

"Hey, be careful," Dustin said. "The outfit's on loan from NYU."

"I don't care if it's on loan from the Smithsonian."

"I should explain," said Wyatt. "I'm doing a documentary on private cooking schools, exclusive ones like this that don't advertise. If ABC is paying half a million for an exposé on the in restaurants of New York, then one of the other networks should be delighted to pick up my *Truth Behind the Pots* for two hundred and fifty thou."

It struck Sonni that he'd come a long way since ladies' douches.

"I wish I'd known earlier that you worked here. I could have saved myself the five bucks I gave my researcher for this tip." He looked around. "Interesting décor."

"Look, I think—" Sonni began.

"I know what you think. You think we have a lot to talk about and that we should sit down and do it. And you're absolutely right. But not now. I have a shot at an Emmy with this idea, because it's not going to be a puff job. People get ripped off at these places—not all of them, of course—but I've heard of one where they pay a hundred bucks just to learn how to make an *omelette*. A hundred bucks! Can you believe that?"

Sonni nodded. Her stomach felt queasy.

"Say . . . you're not a company girl, are you?"

"Huh?" she stiffened.

"A company girl. You know, won't say anything unless the boss approves?"

"Oh—oh, no." Sonni relaxed.

"Good. Then you can tell me about the school as we walk around. Follow us, Dustin, and get it all. We'll cut later."

Dustin drew a bead on Sonni. The camera's red light was on.

"Wait a minute." Sonni held her hand in front of her face. "I'm terrible at interviews. You, um, should really speak to the owner."

"Is she around?"

"Er . . . yes and no."

"I don't understand."

Sonni began speaking rapidly. "Well, when she's here, yes; when she's not, no. But then she never gives interviews anyway, so I suppose it would sort of be pointless for you to talk to her."

"Never gives interviews, eh?" Wyatt sucked in his cheek knowingly. He signaled Dustin to continue shooting.

Sonni accelerated. "That's what makes our school so exclusive. Nobody really knows about it, except of course the people who cook here, and they don't talk about it because they're either cooking or eating." She shrugged, forced a smile. Why hadn't anyone ever perfected teleportation? Mexico would be lovely right now.

"You're a little nervous," Wyatt said softly. "Veracity is the only way I'll cash in on a documentary, so just act natural."

Dustin moved in for a closeup, and Sonni drew back. "Does he have to aim that thing right at me?"

"Relax. Pretend he's a fly on the wall."

Sonni failed to find the image comforting.

Wyatt patted her hand. "Maybe you'd feel better seated," he said. "I'll shut off the TV and we can turn this couch right around like so— Oh. Excuse me."

Evelyn stared and blinked. Her mouth was slightly open, and her head lolled to the side. The blond wig she'd been wearing had come askew. She looked like a discarded oversized Barbie doll.

"Oh no," she said dazedly waving her hand. "Not ready to go . . . too young . . ."

"I beg your pardon?" He looked at Sonni. "What's she talking about?"

"Uh, the *wine*. She means the wine is too young, too early to drink. Evelyn's the school's wine expert. She's on her break now."

"Not with sausages," Evelyn whimpered.

Sonni lowered her voice, led Wyatt away. "She's had a hard day. Four of the Bordeaux she selected weren't ready."

"I'd like to talk to her."

"Maybe you can come back another night when—"

At that moment, Joanna burst from the kitchen giggling. She was wearing Agnelli's bulletproof vest.

"Hey, come on in," she called. "You're missing all the—"

"*Food*," said Sonni quickly, jumping in front of Dustin's camera. "It's what all of us here at What's Cooking are concerned about. *Aren't we, Miss J?*"

Joanna eyed Wyatt and Dustin, looked quizzically at Sonni.

"Mr. Stelson has made a *surprise* visit to film our *cooking class* in action. He's doing a documentary." Sonni stepped back and pinched Joanna's arm.

"Ow . . . Oh, how nice." Joanna had the look of a figure skater going downstream on an ice floe.

"That's a rather interesting garment you're wearing," Wyatt observed. "Some sort of apron?"

"Er . . . well, yes. It's a lobster bib."

"Lobster bib?"

"You know, for when the lobsters are live and you're trying to put them into the pot? This protects the students from scratches." Joanna made her hand into a claw to demonstrate.

"Aren't lobsters pegged to prevent that?"

"Not the ones on sale."

"That's news to me," Wyatt said.

"Probably to a lot of people," Joanna assured him. "Nice talking to you." She shot a glance at Sonni and then tore back to the kitchen. Wyatt started after her.

Sonni grabbed his arm. "You can't go in there now."

"Why not?"

"Because they're making a soufflé. Those things fall just like that."

"We won't make a sound."

"You don't understand. A hiccup could mean disaster." There was a crash from the kitchen.

"Fuckin' bats," someone shouted.

Sonni suddenly wished she were dead.

Wyatt raised an accusing eyebrow. "I'd say that about did it for the soufflé. Go on, Dustin."

"No, wait!" Sonni grabbed Dustin's belt.

"I hate to say this, Sonni," said Wyatt, "but I suspect you're trying to hide something."

"No . . . no." It wasn't a lie; she was trying to hide everything.

"I can understand an employee's protective feeling for an employer, but the public deserves protection, too. They deserve the truth. Honesty is what human love is all about. It's all I've ever asked of everyone." Wyatt gazed at her with half-lowered lids. "It's all I've ever wanted from someone. I suppose that's why I'm the People's Person. I'd like you to understand. Do you?"

Sonni had forgotten how blue his eyes were, how strong

his features were, how much he stood for everything she believed in. She had even forgotten why she hated him. "Yes," she murmured, and released Dustin's belt.

"Now can we go to the kitchen?"

She nodded. "But there's something I have to tell you first."

He put two fingers to her lips. "Later. I'm paying Dustin by the hour."

"But—"

It was too late. Wyatt was already in the kitchen. Agnelli had reclaimed his vest from Joanna and was holding it in front of his face. Danziger and Stern had their windbreakers on, collars up, and they were wearing sunglasses. The girls had all put on wigs.

"Hey, no cameras," Agnelli bellowed. "Can't you see we're trying to cook?" He grabbed a bowl and tossed in two eggs and began to beat them. The shells were still on.

Joanna smiled at Wyatt. "They, um, add body. We strain them out later."

"Yeah," Agnelli said.

Wyatt looked skeptical. "May I ask you, sir, why you're holding your lobster bib like that?"

"My *what*?"

"We allow the students to do whatever they like with their bibs," Joanna said quickly. "Some wear them, some hold them. It depends on how they're going to deal with the lobster."

"Look," Agnelli said. "This is our first lesson. Why don't you wait until we're more prepared?"

"And spoil the *verité*. Oh, no. If I gave advance warning, I'd get actors, not cooking students. Most people act differently when they know they're going to be on television."

"Television?"

"Network, I hope. In fact, I'll need you to sign a release." Wyatt pulled one from his attaché case and handed it to Agnelli, who promptly tore it up. "Oh, camera shy, eh?" Wyatt smiled. "I guess there's one in every crowd."

"Well, guess again, 'cause there are four in this one." Agnelli put on his vest. "Come on, guys, let's go." Danziger and Stern were already out the door. "Hey, Briggs!"

"Just let me flip this. I think I've got the hang of it." Briggs was grinning and holding his pan in front of Dustin's camera.

"Are you crazy?" Agnelli screamed.

"I've never been on television."

"You've never been on suspension either, though you've sure as hell tried." Agnelli grabbed his partner's arm. The pan fell to the floor.

"You've ruined my omelette."

"I'm saving your job."

"All right, all right. But I don't know why we always have to do things your way."

"Because," said Agnelli, "you're an asshole. Now let's *move.*"

Wyatt said nothing as they left, then turned to Sonni. "Those guys weren't students, were they?" His voice was somber.

Sonni shook her head.

"And that *wasn't* a lobster bib, was it?"

She shook her head again.

"What sort of cooking school is this?" he asked.

And she told him.

Wyatt listened attentively. He ignored the sounds of arriving customers and didn't seem to notice when Ernie climbed in from the fire escape through the kitchen window, nor when Karen slipped Dustin a menu and they both disappeared. Occasionally, he made a note on a three-by-five index card. When Sonni finished, he walked across the kitchen tapping the edge of the card on his teeth.

"But you do cook and serve food here, right?"

Sonni blinked. It was like confessing to a murder and then having someone ask you about your tennis game. "Well, yes," she said, bewildered, "but only omelettes."

"*Only* omelettes, she says." Wyatt shook his head in disbelief. "It wouldn't matter if it were only hot dogs. Don't you understand that your sink's not stainless steel, your dishwasher doesn't have a sanitizer? There's no exit sign, no fire extinguisher. Rules of basic hygiene can't be enforced, since every Tom, Dick and Harry gets to beat his own eggs—and these baseball bats are not only a danger, they're a fire hazard. My God, Sonni, hasn't anyone considered the fines you could be hit with if a Health Department official came up here?"

Sonni admitted that no one had.

"And you've got a cat in here, too, for Christ's sake." Mouse was sprawled beside the food processor. Wyatt flicked at her tail with the index card. There was no response. "Paralyzed?"

" 'Luded out."

"*What*?" He recoiled, horrified.

Sonni suddenly felt better. Wyatt considered the taking of anything stronger than an aspirin as mainlining; he'd once denounced pharmacists as pushers. "You know," she said, "from too many 'Ludes."

"You give her *Quaaludes*?"

"Only when she's wired from too much coke. She can do lines longer than those that used to be in front of Studio 54."

"Oh." He nodded. "For a moment there I thought you were serious. In my business, you meet all kinds."

"In mine too," Sonni said, and instantly regretted her competitiveness.

"Look, Sonni," Wyatt said earnestly, "I didn't mean to lash out like that, but regulations aren't established for the hell of it. They're made to protect the most vulnerable segment of our society, the defenseless public—innocent children, pregnant women—"

"Our only customers are men."

"That's a violation already. Discrimination."

Sonni began to remember why she hated him. It was time to change positions. "So what happened to your hair?" she asked.

"It's gone."

"I've noticed."

Wyatt ran his hand over his head. "It's a long story."

"I'd be interested in hearing it sometime."

"Okay." He picked up a menu from the counter, studied it a moment. "How about after a Lollipop in brunette with a side of foreplay?"

In the bedroom, Wyatt said, "You know, I didn't figure you for a pro when we met. No offense, but I thought you were just an ordinary pickup. I suppose I should have known when you filched that hundred."

"Filched!" Sonni cried. "Of all the—"

"Hey, don't get me wrong. I'm not saying that you weren't worth it. As I recall, you were a marvelous lay. If you want to know the truth, I've been with women who've charged twice what you did and I never even got off. I just feel that you should have let me know beforehand."

"Wait a minute. You mean . . . you didn't leave me that money because you thought I was a hooker?"

"I may be the People's Person, but I'm not Santa Claus. I thought you were . . . hell, just a nice woman."

Sonni's hands dropped limply to her lap. "I was—I mean I still am, but . . ."

"Look, there's nothing wrong with being a call girl as long as you're honest about it."

Sonni shook her head slowly. "I didn't take the hundred."

"You didn't?"

"It must have fallen out of your wallet."

Wyatt snapped his fingers. "Son of a gun! You might be right. I'll bet that's how I lost my American Express card last week." He took out his wallet and shook it; a bill fell out. "That's it, all right. I'm buying a new one first thing tomorrow."

Dazed, Sonni murmured, "I don't believe it."

"Well, I am," he said.

"You don't understand."

"*I* don't understand?" He reacted as if such a possibility was unthinkable. "I don't understand what?"

"That what I saw as Destiny's Design was only your crummy wallet."

"Crummy? Listen, maybe the seam's ripped, but this is genuine pigskin. I've just finished an investigation of several so-called *leather* manufacturers, and I've already nailed two who were using vinyl and calling it man-made leather."

"Swell," she said numbly.

"Hey, you're really upset. I'll tell you what. I'm going to forget about the hundred. How about that? We'll . . . call it even." He unbuckled his belt. "You really ought to ask management to supply hangers. Permanent press is much more temporary than people are led to believe. Customers could wind up looking like Bowery bums getting free meals here."

"I'm management," she said, surprised that he hadn't understood that from her earlier explanation.

"You?" He looked shocked and impressed. Sonni didn't know whether to be flattered because he thought her too innocent to run such an operation, or offended because he thought her too stupid.

"What I mean," he continued, "is that this is big-time stuff. I just assumed some sharp businessmen were behind it."

"Nope. Just a couple of working girls."

"No outside backers?"

"Just a lucky break." She neglected to say that the break had been in his wallet. "And a lot of diligence, hard work, patience, nights of burning the midnight oil, grabbing opportunity when it knocked, sacrifice, battling the odds, and getting down on our hands and knees when necessary."

Near Boo-Boo Palmetto's photo on the bureau, a small yellow bulb began to flash.

"What's that?" Wyatt asked.

"Our latest addition. It's for efficiency. It means you're supposed to have come already and that your omelette is ready to cook." Sonni began to button up.

"But I didn't get my Lollipop," Wyatt protested.

"We'll have to leave and go around again, or else it throws everyone off schedule." She used the example of people bunching up at the bottom of an escalator.

Reluctantly, Wyatt put on his pants.

"But because of the inconvenience, you're entitled to

additional complimentary foreplay," she said. "It's house
policy."

Forty-five minutes later they were back in the bedroom
and Sonni was removing her bra.

"It might be nice if you had music," Wyatt said, "and
profitable too. I've read that it stimulates consumers."

"Some franchisees like it, but it's optional. I find that it
throws customers. They tend to keep time with it. A polka
would be disconcerting, and something like "The Minute
Waltz" could ruin everything."

"You have a point." Wyatt stretched out on the bed.

Sonni looked at her watch; a pilot checking gauges before takeoff. She was naked. Wyatt was naked. All systems
were go. She taxied provocatively toward him.

"You look great," he said.

"Thanks." She began fondling his toes, then flicked her
tongue across the underside of his knees. When she
reached his thighs, he grabbed her breasts, threw her over,
and climbed on top.

"I want to change my order," he said.

"Have it your way," she said.

He did.

Sonni had almost forgotten how good an old-fashioned
Yankee–Red Sox game could be—even with a man she
hated.

Later, eating his omelette, Wyatt explained the reason
for his baldness. It was a long story, so long, in fact, that by
the time he was finished the sun was up, and tiny bristles
had begun to sprout on his chin in ironic mockery of his
head's shiny surface.

It was a terrible tale of savagery, calculated vengeance,

and a good man wronged. Wyatt didn't omit a single detail, which was why it took so long, took nine hours. If he had wanted to, he could have recounted the whole story in less than a minute.

What had happened was this: He had attacked a shampoo manufacturer who claimed his product could "tame the wildest locks." A short time later he received anonymously, a sample bottle of a new shampoo that guaranteed to remove dandruff forever. Finding the claim dubious, he tried the sample, suffering as he did from occasional scalp flakiness. To his horror, the bottle had contained a depilatory. It removed all his hair and damaged the follicles irreparably. But the worst part, the part at which he'd broken into tears recounting, was that the label on the bottle had been accurate: He'd never have dandruff again.

Sonni stroked his head and experienced the odd sensation of petting a globe or a honeydew melon. And it felt good. Real. Hair, she realized, was deceptive, a cosmetic to make people look younger or older, richer or tougher, taller or smarter. Cops grew it to go undercover. Soldiers cut it to keep in step. Men and women dyed, bleached, and styled it to change jobs, mates, minds and sex. There was something incomparably *honest* about baldness.

She tried to console Wyatt with this, by pointing out how much money he'd save since he'd never need a cut, how he wouldn't ever have to worry about where he left his brush or comb, how he'd conserve energy by not using a blow dryer, how much more room he'd have in his bathroom without the clutter of shampoos and conditioners. When none of these seemed to lift his spirits, she made him a cup of coffee and gave him a Lollipop.

The Lollipop did it. He left around noon, humming and happy.

Sonni went into the study to get her purse and was surprised to find Ernie there. He looked beat, looked as if he'd just marched from Phnom Penh to Saigon. A glance in the mirror told her that she didn't look much better herself.

"I thought everyone had gone home," she said.

"So did I. But when I saw you were still with a customer, I figured I'd better hang out."

"That wasn't necessary."

"Neither was climbing the fire escape to get back in, but I've learned it's better to play it safe." He emptied his ashtray into a wastebasket. "Who was the guy?"

"An old friend."

"Oh."

"We had a lot to talk about."

"I imagine so," said Ernie.

He took her downstairs and hailed a taxi. He told her to go home and get some rest.

"You look like shit," he said.

Only when Sonni was in bed and about to drift off to sleep did she realize that it was the first time Ernie Hemmingway had ever noticed how she looked.

Chapter 17

"How about dinner and the theater?" Wyatt asked, phoning the next day. "Dustin can't borrow the camera again for a while, so I'm putting myself on holiday."

"I have to work."

"Every night?" He was disappointed.

"Just about. There are four big conventions in town and we've been shorthanded all week."

"Oh." He paused. "I'd really like to see you."

"I'd really like to see *you*," Sonni said, and meant it. Her night with him had erased all her nurtured antagonism. His courage in facing the world bald was an inspiration, a testament to his integrity. His honesty was an aphrodisiac.

"Why don't you come to the school?" she suggested.

"Well, to be quite truthful, I had a less expensive evening in mind."

"If you stop to think about it, dinner and a show would cost more."

"Hmmm." There was a long silence, then a number of muted clicks that sounded like a calculator. "Okay," he said. "I'll see you around eight."

She was excited and found herself humming for the rest of the day. It was almost like scoring the winning run when she had pinch-hit for Barry Zilkman in the seventh grade; almost like decking The Shem.

Amazingly, it was almost like being in love.

When her father called later that afternoon, she found herself giggling as she said hello.

"Are you all right?" he asked.

"I've never felt better," she said. "What's up?"

"Are you sitting down?"

She had never liked that question. "Yes . . . why?"

"Because I have something to tell you. I'm getting out of the novelty business."

"Daddy!"

"My mind's made up."

"But . . . but your Dinky . . ."

"Forget my Dinky. It's just another Hula-Hoop. It's time for me to settle down in a real job, something that will provide me with a sense of accomplishment as well as fringe benefits; something where I can feel that I'm serving a purpose as well as myself."

Sonni was stunned. "A job? What job?"

"Well," he said, "I was thinking about vice-president, quality control, based at your Miami school."

"*Daddy!*" She held the receiver away from her and stared at it. "That's . . . ridiculous."

"What's ridiculous? All the best franchises have them. Listen to me, Son, a little nepotism never hurt. It makes smart business sense to keep certain things in the family."

Sonni was about to protest, then started to laugh. Why not? she thought. "Why not!" she said.

"That's my girl," said Irv Mishkin.

When he hung up, Sonni decided she'd done the right thing. Her father wasn't ready to retire, he liked Miami— and, if nothing else, he was still able to appreciate a good omelette.

Wyatt appeared at What's Cooking at eight on the dot. Sonni, who'd been anxiously anticipating his arrival, took one look and gasped. His head, which less than twenty-four hours ago had been naked as a light bulb, was flowing with hair, long cream-colored straggly hair, parted in the center and framing his face like afghan hound ears.

"What do you think?" he asked, tossing his head so that his locks fell gracefully across his shoulders.

Sonni was speechless.

"Pull it," he said.

"Huh?"

"My hair. Come on, pull it."

Sonni was too stunned not to. Wyatt yelped.

"How about that?" he said. "Sewn on and guaranteed for ten years. I know I probably overcompensated, but at this length I can get it cut three, maybe four times before I have to say goodbye to my barber forever."

"Wow!" Karen said, joining them, pointing at Wyatt. "That's remarkable."

"Feels like the real thing, too," he said. "Pull it."

Karen shrugged and yanked.

Wyatt winced. "What did I tell you?"

"Great," she said, "but I was talking about the resemblance. It's unbelievable. Don't you see it, Sonni?"

"See what?" Sonni wasn't seeing anything too clearly at
the moment.

"Oh, come on. Are you blind? Here—" Karen pushed
the sides of Wyatt's hair forward—"now whom does he
look like?"

"General Custer?" Wyatt offered, bemused and
pleased with the attention.

Sonni admitted that he did look like someone.

"Someone?" Karen exclaimed. "You *are* blind." She
waved Evelyn over.

"Sir Lancelot, perhaps?" said Wyatt.

"What's up?" said Evelyn warily. She nodded to Wyatt,
then did a double take and stared. For a moment it
seemed she might faint.

Karen folded her arms smugly. "Look like anyone?"

"Oh my God!"

Wyatt's eyes widened. "Jesus?"

"Boo-Boo Palmetto," Evelyn murmured reverently. It
was said that she'd lost her virginity to one of Bob Dylan's
roadies and had never gotten over the Woodstock festi-
val.

"Boo-Boo Palmetto?" Wyatt looked puzzled and disappointed. "Who's he?"

"He *was* a rock star," said Sonni, acknowledging the
resemblance.

Karen went to find a photograph.

"Was?" said Wyatt. "What's he now?"

"Dead."

"Here," said Karen. She handed Wyatt the same
framed photo of Boo-Boo and Reggie Jackson that was in
all the bedrooms. "That's Boo-Boo."

Wyatt studied the picture, then looked at himself in the

mirror. "I thought I'd seen myself someplace before when I left the doctor's office. Damn! I'll have to cut it right away. I can't see making money as a consumer advocate looking like a dead rock star."

"Maybe not," said Karen, "but you could probably make more money as a dead rock star than looking like a consumer advocate. Just ask Fletcher." She indicated the short dark-haired man wearing a pair of diamond-speckled gold dice on a chain around his neck who was talking to Joanna. "He makes millions managing a whole mortuary of them."

"Millions? For dead rock stars?"

"Well, they're not all dead and they're not all rock stars—though the biggest money-makers are. He handles celebrity impersonators."

"Millions?" Wyatt looked thoughtful; looked at the photo. He brushed his hair forward, then held the photograph next to his face in front of the mirror. "Son of a gun," he said. "Boo-Boo Palmetto." He asked Sonni to introduce him to Mr. Fletcher.

"What for?"

"The hell of it," he said, but Sonni began to feel uneasy. Wyatt was still holding the photograph as they approached Fletcher.

"Excuse me, Arthur," Sonni said, tapping Fletcher on the shoulder. "I'd like you to meet someone."

"You make the introductions, baby, and I'll make the deals." Fletcher extended his hand automatically, then froze. "Well, I'll be . . . That's phenomenal. This guy looks just like—" He snapped his fingers, trying to think.

"Yes?" Wyatt said eagerly.

"Do me a favor. Flatten your hair and push it all the way back."

"Push it *back?*"

"Yeah, yeah. All the way."

Wyatt put the photograph between his knees and used both hands. "Like this?"

"That's it! Man, with the right haircut, you could be a dead ringer for that consumer advocate Stelson—you know, the People's Person?"

"He *is* the People's Person," said Sonni.

"No! What rotten luck. The variety shows are crying for straight look-alikes." Fletcher patted Wyatt's shoulder. "Nice to meet you, buddy. For a moment there I was seeing six-figure dollar signs. Sorry."

"But I'd go on a variety show," said Wyatt.

"Nothing personal, but who'd want you? Celebrity impersonators are bankable. There's nothing bankable about a consumer advocate." Fletcher turned back to Joanna.

"Hold it," Wyatt said. He pulled the photograph from between his knees. "Do you know who this is?"

"Sure. Reggie Jackson."

"No. Him." Wyatt pointed.

"Of course. Boo-Boo Palmetto."

"Okay." Wyatt handed Sonni the picture and quickly brushed his hair toward his face. He put his arm around Sonni the way Boo-Boo's was around Reggie Jackson in the photograph. "Take a look at this."

"Hmmm," said Fletcher.

"Boo-Boo used to slump more," said Evelyn.

Wyatt lowered his shoulders.

"More. You know, sort of like an ape with stomach cramps."

Wyatt hunched over. "Like this?"

"Let your arms just dangle. That's it."

"Hmmm . . . hmmmm," said Fletcher. "Interesting. Can you handle a guitar?"

"I used to fool around with my father's banjo."

"It's how you look with it that counts."

"Well . . ." Wyatt went to the bookcase and picked up one of Boo-Boo's baseball bats and started to strum it. "How's this?"

"Lean to the side a bit and bob your head," said Karen.

"I think he's got it," said Evelyn. "Loosen your shoulders a little. Pump your pelvis."

"Really, Wyatt," Sonni said, "don't you think this has gone far enough?" He was hunched over, strumming the bat, twitching and gyrating with his mouth agape in such a fashion that he looked as if he'd just swallowed a baseball and was being given the Heimlich maneuver by the ghost of Boo-Boo Palmetto.

"He might be only beginning," said Fletcher. "I'm seeing potential."

"Potential?" Wyatt said. "Watch this." He raised the bat above his head and leaped up on the coffee table, began strumming again.

"Getting warmer," said Fletcher.

"What do you mean, warmer?" Wyatt said, his face flushed. "I'm hot, man." The doorbell rang. "Don't anybody move," he cried, "Boo-Boo Palmetto will answer that."

He jumped from the table and, still clutching the bat, flung open the door. "What's cooking?" he drawled.

A shrill, terrified scream pierced the apartment. *"Boo-Boo!"*

Sonni stared. A handsomely dressed dark-haired woman in a tailored oxford gray suit clutched the doorframe, then staggered into the room.

Joanna reached the distraught woman first and helped Wyatt ease her into a chair. There was nothing about her that was familiar, but as Sonni approached she knew she'd seen the woman before—and in that chair.

"Who is she?" asked Wyatt. He was awkwardly massaging her wrists.

"I think," said Sonni slowly, "that she's Boo-Boo's widow."

"The ultimate litmus test!" Wyatt cried. "I'm in. I'm in!" He flung down her hands and headed for Fletcher.

"Ta'Shi?" Sonni asked hesitantly.

The woman nodded weakly.

"You look so . . . different," Sonni stammered. "We didn't expect you back for at least another year."

"Neither did I," Ta'Shi said, "but I never left." Her plane had been delayed in taking off, and while waiting in the lounge she'd met a lawyer who she felt certain was her soul mate from an earlier life. "It was an incredible cosmic coincidence. When he began telling me how he'd learned to cope emotionally with tax problems, keep his spirits up when the market was down, just live on his yacht when city pressures became too much, I realized that this man had more to offer my universal essence than Guru Baktawanda. We went back to his apartment that night and were married last month."

"Ta'Shi, that's wonderful."

"I'm Pandora Palmetto-Bowles now. Evan's given me a whole new appreciation of old values. I feel reborn. I've discovered there's meaning to a good name, a good Dun and Bradstreet rating, things that so many people never even think about. I only came over tonight because I've learned the importance of written lease agreements." She opened her purse and handed a document to Sonni. "Evan drew this up. It's for three years, but I'm sure if you wanted it for five, or ten, even twenty, we could work it out."

"I think twenty would be pushing it," said Sonni, "but thanks for the option."

"I'm sorry I screamed," Pandora said, "but when I saw that man with the long hair holding a bat the same way Boo did when he used to answer the door, I felt—" she bit her lip as it began to tremble— "as if my entire rebirth had just gone down the toilet."

"I understand," said Sonni. It was time to have a serious talk with Wyatt.

He was handing Fletcher a pen as she approached. "You're sure about that?" she heard him say.

"Sure?" Fletcher chuckled. "I handle the biggest celebrity impersonators in the country. I've got two Elvises, a Janis Joplin, a Jimi Hendrix, and a Bobby Darin on tour right now. Tabernacle Mania is booked solid for the holidays. I'm telling you, you'll be cooling a million next year."

"Even though I can't sing?"

"Who can? It's all lip sync these days. Even the live ones use it." Fletcher returned Wyatt's pen and held out his hand. "A shake is good enough for me. I'll have the contracts ready tomorrow. You'll be my first Boo-Boo. Glad to have you aboard."

"Aye, aye," said Wyatt. He gave a mock salute with the bat.

Sonni gripped Wyatt's arm. "But you can't!"

"Of course he can," said Fletcher.

"Why can't I?" said Wyatt.

"Because . . . because . . ." Sonni felt everything coming apart, just as it had come together—like cake removed too early from the oven. "Because you'll be wearing another man's clothes, singing another man's songs, and making money by using another man's fans. It's out-and-out deceit!"

"There's nothing deceitful about being out and out,' said Wyatt.

"But your whole life is predicated on honesty," she protested. "You're the People's Person."

"One of my Elvises is a former priest," said Fletcher.

"There," said Wyatt, "if a man of God can do it, why not a man of the people? I mean, it's not as if I'm saying I *am* Palmetto, is it? There's a difference between a fake and an *honest* fake. Besides, my building is going co-op, and I need the money. Besides that, I—"

Sonni could listen to no more. She turned and fled. Wyatt followed her. When he reached her at the far end of the hall near the bathroom, she was crying.

"Hey, look at me." He turned her around. "You didn't let me finish. What I was going to say was that I can use the money because I want to get married."

"Married?" Sonni felt as if she'd swallowed six raw omelettes. She thought she was going to be sick.

"Yes. To you."

She blinked. "Are you asking me to marry you?"

"I wanted it to be a surprise."

"It is," she admitted, "but what's that have to do with money?"

"Well, I don't want my wife to . . . to have to work. I mean, I don't think there's anything wrong with What's Cooking—except you really should get a stainless-steel sink—but other people might. You know how other people are. You have to understand that I'm always going to be in the public eye—and I want you with me." He tilted her chin and kissed her gently. "Of course, if you can keep your interest and still draw from the place without anyone being able to prove it, that would be different."

Sonni just stared at him.

"You don't have to give me your answer right now. Whenever you're ready, just surprise me."

"I'm ready," she said, and surprised him by telling him to fuck off.

"It's late and you've drunk too much already."

Sonni, who had been sitting alone in the study, looked up, but there was no one there. Then she saw Ernie in the doorway.

"Oh, it's you," she said. She took another sip of her Scotch. "What do you want?"

"I want to go home," he said.

"So go."

"I don't want to leave you here."

"Looks like you've got a problem, then. I'll go home when I'm good and ready." She downed her drink.

"You're good and you're ready." He helped her to her feet. "Come on."

"You don't understand," she said, holding Ernie's shoulder. "I thought I loved him."

"I thought clouds were whipped cream. We all grow up." He put his arm around her waist.

"I feel like shit."

"You don't look a hell of a lot better."

"I could have been an anchorperson if I'd said yes to Drury."

"I could have been a Rockefeller if my mother had said yes to John D."

"Is that the truth?"

"The truth is just a lie someone believes in until he doesn't believe in it anymore."

"Like being innocent until proven guilty?"

"Sort of."

"Like Vietnam?"

"Like DDT, cigarettes, Nixon, a lot of things."

Sonni scratched her head, thought for a moment. "Like a bunt?"

"Like a bunt."

He led her out into the hall, locked the door, and pressed the elevator button.

"I'm not as drunk as you think," Sonni said. Ernie caught her as she stumbled forward. "Then again, maybe I am."

Outside on Park Avenue Ernie put both arms around her as they waited for a cab.

"Can we have sex?" she said.

"This is no time to think about work."

"I'm not thinking about work, I'm thinking about sex."

Ernie hailed a taxi. "We'll see," he said, helping her in.

"That's what my father used to say, 'We'll see.' He always used to say that when I asked him if I could do things like go to the movies or go roller-skating. He'd say, 'We'll see.' Never yes or no, always 'We'll see.' "

"What did the we'll see turn out to mean?"

"Sometimes it meant yes, sometimes no. When he smiled it was yes. What did yours mean?"

"We'll see," said Ernie, and he smiled.

Inside Sonni's apartment Ernie helped her onto the bed and took off her shoes.

"Do I look terrible?"

"Terrible."

"Am I really drunk?"

"Polluted."

"I don't know whether I want to cry or throw up."

"If those are the choices, cry." He went into the

bathroom and brought her a cold washcloth, placed it on her forehead.

"Ernie?"

"What?"

"I want to open more cooking schools."

"Not tonight."

"Do you think there's something wrong with a woman who's chosen a career based on having intimate physical contact with men for money? I mean, do you think she's bad?"

"No."

"Really?"

"Really. My mother was a urologist, specialized in prostate problems for over twenty-five years. That's pretty intimate. My father adored her. They both kept their careers separate from their marriage."

"What was your father?"

"A gynecologist." He began massaging Sonni's neck.

"That feels good," Sonni said. "Thank you."

"Don't mention it. It's against my principles to have sex with a drunken woman." He lay down beside her. "Unless, of course, I happen to be in love with her."

"Ernie, is that the truth?"

"If not, may God strike me impotent."

It was, to their mutual delight, the whole truth, and nothing but.

It was also one hell of a great ball game.